VIKING ACADEMY

VIKING ACADEMY: BOOK ONE

S.T. BENDE

Viking Academy
Viking Academy: Book One
Copyright © 2019, S.T. Bende
Edited by: CREATING ink
Cover Art by: Alerim
Map by: BZN Studio Designs

First publication: 2019, S.T. Bende

DEDICATION

*To Olaug—thank you for showing me those rocks in Norway
. . . and for sharing a friendship that's timeless.*

CHAPTER 1

GET OVER IT, SAGA. Cold water never hurt anybody.

Maybe not. But as I stood at the edge of Norway's North Sea, dead tired and shivering in the early morning breeze, I wanted nothing more than to climb back into bed and sleep off my late night. As we always did on the last evening of summer, my cousins and I had hung out by the campfire until well past midnight. And, in typical Skånstad family fashion, I was the only one of us who'd dragged her butt out of bed for a morning swim.

Routines died hard with me.

Just get it over with already. You're making it worse by putting it off.

Icy water lapped my goose-pimpled legs as I held my breath and waded into the frosty cove. With a nod at Steinar, the only other nutjob crazy enough to swim at six a.m. on a perfectly good Friday, I pulled my goggles over my eyes and dove in.

I was immediately filled with regret.

It took a solid fifty strokes before my skin acclimated to the cold, and another fifty before I could breathe without wincing. But eventually I fell into a rhythm, making my way toward the little island just offshore, one stroke at a time. By the time I reached my marker and doubled back, my breathing was steady, my body temperature was several degrees above miserable, and my thoughts had shifted from *good God, it's freaking cold!* to *I wish it wasn't my last day here.*

I cherished my summers at the cabin—the early morning swims, the afternoon lefse baking with my grandmother/guardian, Mormor, and the late-night deck-side Monopoly matches with my cousins. Our trips had been a family tradition long before my parents died, but this one was special—it was my last before starting college. My flight home departed in twenty-six hours, and by next week, I'd be rooming with my cousin Olivia, studying international relations and earning out my archery scholarship at Northern Minnesota University. For a school that was just a few hours' drive from our hometown, it felt like it was worlds away. Everything about my life was about to change.

As a girl who appreciated predictability, I had mixed feelings about this.

I turned my head to the side, drawing a breath as I neared the shore. Mormor always made a huge breakfast on the last day of our trips—Norsk waffles, bacon, fruit, eggs. And coffee.

God willing, she'd made *all* the coffee.

With a final stroke, I lifted my head and lowered my feet. My toes dug into coarse sand as I waded to shore. When the sand gave way to rocks, I stepped more cautiously . . . and yelped when I jammed my toe into an unexpected protrusion.

"*Skit*," I swore, reaching down to rub my foot. My fingers brushed against a smooth, sharp surface, and I stilled.

That was no rock.

Wrenching my goggles off my head, I bent down to study the crystal-clear water. Air whistled through my teeth as I sucked in a breath.

Holy. Freaking. Mother.

I bent lower and placed my hand around the thick, leather hilt of what appeared to be a dagger—a dirty, age-worn dagger, that was wedged firmly between two surprisingly immobile rocks. When my tugging proved futile, I wrapped my goggles around my wrist and used both hands to pry the blade free. It took a solid minute, during which my body temperature dropped back down to miserable, but with one fierce yank, I landed on my butt in the ocean, stubborn dagger firmly in hand.

All the coffee, Mormor. Please.

I scanned the area for additional weapons because apparently, ocean weapons were a thing now. Finding none, I made my way to the shore, rested the dagger across my palms, and took in every detail. It looked really old—the handle was well worn, and though the blade was badly tarnished, it bore a few dirty gems, and what looked like runic etchings. Runic etchings? How old was this thing? And moreover, who threw a dagger into the ocean? Kids swam here. I swam here! Sure, beach people were all kinds of laid-back, but seriously. *Who threw a dagger in the ocean?*

I glanced up toward my grandmother's cabin. The light was on in the little kitchen, which meant Mormor was likely puttering around, manifesting my coffee dreams into reality. She lived for history—she'd worked our family tree all the way back to one thousand A.D., and she had a basement filled with family heirlooms that went as far back as the 1800s. She would be all over this dagger . . . after she and my eco-warrior cousin ripped into the perp who'd littered in their precious ocean. Olivia and I were born three days apart, and she'd been my closest friend since the day I moved in with my grandmother—just two doors down from my cousin's house. We'd been looking forward to rooming together since we'd gotten our acceptance letters to NMU. Just one more week . . .

I transferred the dagger to one hand and held it overhead, hoping to catch Mormor's attention. Or Olivia's, if she'd dragged her butt out of bed yet. But the moment I raised the blade, my knuckles tightened around the hilt and my elbow locked at my ear. The cabin wavered in and out of focus as the beach spun in a dizzying circle that left my stomach churning.

What the hell was happening? And, more importantly, how did I make it stop?

My knees buckled and I took a step back. As the beach spun faster, I stepped again. And again. I was calf-deep in the sea when dizziness finally won. My knees hit the water, then crashed hard on the rocks in a moment of bone-searing agony. I started to double over, whether to throw up or pass out I hadn't determined, but my arm may as well have been soldered to my ear. Now the dagger was vibrating, its intense pulses making my arms shake to the point of exhaustion.

The dagger had to go.

I flexed my hand, willing my fingers to release the wretched relic, but its will was stronger than mine. Switching tactics, I used my free hand to pry my fingers from the hilt, and begged. *Please, please let me go.*

My request was denied.

I wrapped my hand around my wrist in a pointless effort to push the dagger back into the ocean. But its vibrations increased until my entire body trembled. The world gave one final, violent wrench before it shattered. The shoreline literally peeled away, pieces floating upward until I was left in a pure, white void.

Panic seized my throat, making breathing impossible. My lips parted and my chest heaved as I tried to forcibly inhale, but the air simply would not flow. I tried again, and again, but either I'd lost the ability to breathe, or there was no air in this void.

Was this how I was going to die?

Suddenly, the void was replaced by a familiar, *non-spinning* shore. The ocean stretched behind me, the rocky shoreline ahead, and the thick, deciduous forest that had stood behind my grandmother's cabin for at least a thousand years was exactly where it had always been.

But the trees looked different. Shorter.

Shorter? That was impossible. Trees didn't shrink. And daggers didn't have wills of their own. Clearly, I'd over-exerted myself swimming, and was now suffering from hallucinations.

Clearly.

But it wasn't just the trees that were different. The cabin was . . . well, it wasn't. My grandmother's redwood-decked beach house had been replaced with a cluster of huts built from thick logs and covered in grass roofs. The ornately carved front door of one opened to reveal a long-haired man wearing muddy, leather pants. He held his free hand to his eyes as he studied the ocean. The thick muscles of his chest tensed as he let out a fierce cry that sent chills racing up my spine.

"*Inntrengere!*"

I didn't know that word, but it didn't sound good.

"*Inntrengere,*" he shouted again, louder this time.

"Um, *hei!* It's just me! Saga Skånstad, Bertha's granddaughter!" I held my hands in front of my face, but with the dagger still in hand, I failed to neutralize the threat. "I live, uh, right there. Where you are, actually. Only not. So that makes us, kind of neighbors in a—"

"*Inntrengere!*" Leather Pants bellowed again. A dozen new leather-clad longhairs emerged from their huts, each more muscular than the last.

Why aren't they understanding me?

The second I thought it, a ripple passed from the dagger up my arm, rocking my body with a series of jolts. The mumbles of the leather-pantsers were suddenly intelligible; it was as if an invisible translator had slipped into my brain. I hoped it worked on both ends, and they'd be able to understand me, too. I needed them to stop staring at me like they wanted my blood, already.

"Intruders!" the men bellowed, a chorus of doom-sayers banging on their chests and reaching for their swords. These guys kept swords hanging by their front doors?

"I'm not an intruder!" I raised my hands again, then quickly lowered them. *Stupid dagger.* "I'm Saga, and I'm hallucinating, so if you could kindly—"

"Defend the shoreline against the boats!" The first leather-pants shouted.

Boats?

Maybe Steinar's grandsons were out in their kayak, or a fellow early riser was heading out to fish? I glanced over my shoulder, expecting to see one of our neighbors. My heart clenched at the sight of three Viking warships, red and white sails raised, streaming straight for the shore.

7

Oh. My. God.

"Defend!" The leather-clad chorus chimed. They raced from their huts, swords in hand as they made their way to a building at the edge of the settlement. They emerged bearing *even more weapons*—bows and arrows and shields and axes.

And they charged straight for me.

My options were slim. I could swim for the little island offshore—and risk being scooped up by what I seriously doubted were friendly Viking fisher-folk. Or I could run for the forest—and risk being axed by one of the leather-pantsers.

I opted for the latter.

But when I lifted my foot, my legs got tangled in something thick and heavy. I face-planted on the beach with a pain-wracked, "Oomph!" Spitting rocky sand from my mouth, I pushed myself up and tried to run again. This time, I discovered my movement was hindered by a dense, damp fabric.

What the hell am I wearing?

I didn't stop to freak out about whatever quick change had occurred while I'd been sizing up the leather-pantsers. I just hiked up the ridiculously dense skirts of whatever absurd dress I was stuck in, tucked the dagger into the fortuitously placed loop at my belt, and ran like my life depended on it.

In all likelihood, it probably did.

The leather-pantsers charged the shore, hitting the beach as I neared the northern edge of their village. When I reached the tree line, I hid myself behind a trunk and chanced a look back. My breaths came in shallow gasps as the Viking ships struck the ocean floor. Their riders leapt into the shallows, swords drawn, and shields raised. They ran for the beach, water flying as they neared their foes. Swords clashed, arrows flew, and the water ran thick with red. The two clans furiously massacred one another while I stood helpless, clinging to a birch tree.

I'd just escaped my first Viking raid.

And I hadn't even had my coffee yet.

CHAPTER 2

R UN, SAGA. JUST RUN.

The words echoed somewhere deep inside my head—probably the part charged with ensuring I didn't succumb to death by Viking slaughter. Since the murdering was still going strong on the beach, I released my grip on the tree and retreated into the forest.

"Ouch!"

I winced as I leaned against a nearby birch to extract whatever sharp object had pricked my foot—because the universe had gifted me the world's bulkiest dress, but no shoes. Bending over, I carefully removed a rock from my heel, and wiped the blood against the coarse fabric of my gown. A quick scan of the forest revealed a tapestry of fallen branches and an infinite number of angular rocks—a veritable landmine for naked feet. Droplets danced on the leaves, meaning it had recently rained in whatever timeline I'd hallucinated myself into. I could count on a thick layer of mud beneath the razor-rocks, which would make running in this too-long dress doubly difficult.

Super.

"Arugh!"

The cry from the beach reminded me I did *not* have time to strategize—not unless I wanted to meet the wrong end of a broadsword. With a big breath, I gripped my skirt in my hands, turned away from the bloodshed, and ran. Pain shot through my feet with each ill-placed step, but rocks and twigs paled in comparison to the head of an arrow . . . or an axe . . . or whatever other weapons were being brandished behind me. Willing myself forward, I lowered my head and ran faster. I managed to put some distance between myself and the beach before a low snarl stopped me cold.

I dug my heels into the mud and reached out to steady myself against a nearby branch. When the snarl sounded again, I flattened my back against the tree's trunk and held my breath.

There were definitely animals in the woods behind my grandmother's cabin—squirrels, deer, and the occasional moose. But whatever had just made that noise wasn't anything I'd heard before. In fact, it sounded almost like . . .

Another snarl echoed through the woods, followed by a pronounced growl.

Oh, skit.

I peeked around the trunk, and bit down hard on

11

my bottom lip. I did *not* want to scream with a massive bear nearby. Forget being slaughtered by Vikings; death by bear-mauling sounded infinitely more terrifying. Not to mention, infinitely more painful.

My heart jackhammered against my ribs. Tree bark dug into my flesh as I pressed myself against the trunk and let out a silent breath. *Think, Saga!* I'd been camping with my cousins a few times. My uncle always told us to make ourselves really big if we ever ran into a bear. Then pray like mad.

But something told me this bear wouldn't be easily intimidated. He lived with axe-wielding, mass-murdering, enormous Vikings. Weaponless, five foot seven, curly haired me wouldn't be much of a threat. Even if I did wave my arms and cry *roar* like Uncle Jon taught me.

I peeked around the trunk again, trying not to scream at the sight of the beast stalking through the woods. Running was out of the question—at this distance, he'd overtake me in seconds. Climbing the tree was a no-go—I wouldn't make it ten feet up in this stupid dress and besides, couldn't bears climb anyway? And going on the offensive wasn't an option—I didn't have the first clue how to wield a dagger, and while my archery skills were impressive, I was sorely lacking in bows and arrows.

Maybe I could just hallucinate again, and wake up back on the beach. In the real world.

Please?

A feral roar sent my heart rate rocketing again, and

I peeked around the tree to find the bear creeping toward me. *Oh, God. They* can *smell fear*. His head tilted as a silent scream escaped my mouth, and his lips pulled back to reveal pointed fangs. He bent lower to the ground in what looked alarmingly like a hunting crouch, and I knew I was out of options.

I had to run like hell.

My brain was a blank slate of terror as I bent my knees and launched from my hiding spot. Mud squished beneath my toes while I put as much distance between the bear and myself as I could manage. The ground trembled as massive paws thundered atop the earth, and I could have sworn his hot, hungry breath was blowing on my neck. Angry snarls bounced off the trees, each rage-filled roar closer than the last. But I didn't turn around.

I didn't want to see death coming.

I was so focused on survival that I failed to notice the two huge Vikings until I'd plowed right into one. My butt struck the ground with a jarring thud. My hip shrieked with the pain of landing on my dagger's hilt, and my head snapped backward, landing in the mud and sending a nausea-inducing wave of pain across my skull. The sky danced above me, a swirl of leaves and clouds, as a second Viking drew a series of arrows and fired them over my head. A roar from behind let me know he'd hit his target . . . and the ensuing growl and the deafening boom of the beast's fall assured me the bear was no longer my primary threat.

That honor belonged to the axe-wielding leather-pantser towering over me.

The Viking's gravelly voice was quiet as he leaned down and snarled, "Get up."

With the world still spinning and hammers pounding at my temples, getting up was a tall order. I placed a palm to the more pain-wracked side of my head, and tried to roll onto an elbow. The movement sent a fresh wave of dizziness coursing through me, and I flopped back onto the ground with a painful thud.

Ow.

Leather Pants must have mistaken my hesitation for defiance. He wrapped rough fingers around my forearm and wrenched me up. My body screamed in protest, but I dug my toes into the mud and steadied myself. If escape was going to be an option, it would have to happen now . . . not *after* these two dragged me back to Murder Beach.

"Are you from Clan Ragnar?" the Viking barked.

Who?

I snuck a glance at the second Viking, who'd busied himself recovering arrows. "Uh . . ."

"Answer me! Did those thieves send you here?"

Right. Clan Ragnar must have been the intruders in the boats.

The ones lying *dead* on the beach.

Oh, God.

"Nope," I blurted. "Definitely not. I'm not with them. I'm, uh . . ."

A time-traveling hallucinator from the distant future hardly seemed like the answer that would earn my release.

Leather Pants tightened his grip around my wrist and jerked me closer. My nostrils flared at the twin stenches of sweat and old fish. My stomach churned as he placed his hand around my waist.

"Markus," he sneered. "Look at this dress. I think we just captured Clan Ragnar's heir."

"You sure about that?" Markus stalked toward me, abandoning his attempt to retrieve arrows from the bear's carcass.

"This is Ragnar's weapon, *ja*?" Leather-Pants tightened his grip around my waist and tugged. I winced as my belt came undone, loosening the dress at my waist and releasing the dagger from its holder.

"Dunno." Markus pulled the dagger from Leather Pants' hands, and held it up. The once-rusted weapon gleamed against a beam of sunlight; the edges of its formerly-scuffed hilt now sparkling with red and blue jewels. *What the hell?* "But whoever she is, she must be important to have a weapon like this."

"And a dress like this."

My breath hitched as Leather Pants fingered the fabric at my waist. The Viking's muddy, brown eyes clouded over. In that instant, he was infinitely more terrifying than the bear. "If she's not Ragnar's heir, she's of great value to *somebody* in that tribe. Wonder how much she's worth to them."

"Not half as much as she's worth to us." Markus' eyes gleamed. "I haven't been on a raid in months."

"Neither have I." Leather Pants sidled closer, making my gut clench. The Viking's palm tightened around my waist as he forced me to his side. "Chief Olav may have forbidden contact with our own females until Lars selects his bride, but he didn't say anything about captives."

"No." Markus' lips parted in a sneer. He wrapped thick fingers around my loose, blond curls and wrenched my head to the side. "He didn't."

I bit the inside of my cheek to keep from screaming. I already had two brutes to outrun—I didn't need their entire clan knowing where to find me.

Think, Saga. Markus held the dagger just out of my reach . . . not that I'd have been able to wrench it from his iron grasp. I wasn't going to be able to scrap my way out of this one. But if I was lucky, I could outsmart my captors.

I hoped.

"Release me," I ordered, willing my voice to hold steady. "As the rightful heir of Clan Ragnar, I order you to return me to Chief . . . to my Chief. Failure to do so will result in your immediate deaths."

"Oh yeah?" Leather Pants tightened his grip. "At whose hand?"

At the question, a flash of light illuminated the forest. Markus immediately released my hair, and let out a cry. "My gods!"

I turned my head toward the source of the light to

find the dagger glowing brightly in Markus' hand. The beams from its blade shot clear to the treetops. *What the actual hell?*

Never mind, just go with it!

"You will die at my hand," I declared. "Release me or my dagger will, uh, slay you."

"It's burning me!" Markus cried. He shook his wrist, the dagger swinging back and forth in his grip. "Knut, do something!"

"What am I supposed to do?" Leather Pants squeezed my waist so hard, I winced. "Just let it go!"

"I can't!" Markus yelled. "Knut!"

"Release me, Knut," I warned.

"No," Knut growled.

"My arm!" Markus cried again. "It's on fire!"

He wasn't kidding. Golden flames lapped their way up Markus' arm. They danced across his torso, entombing him in a sparkling, yellow orb for what looked like an agonizing moment before consuming him entirely. The Viking's screams of terror pierced the forest as he disappeared in a flaming swirl of dust. The instant he was gone, the dagger clattered onto the mud.

Holy freaking mother. This wasn't just an alternate timeline—this was an alternate universe, *with actual magic.*

"Markus?" Knut shouted.

Now, Saga. Escape now.

"Release me." My voice belied a calm I *so* did not feel. "Or you're next."

Knut's eyes darted between me and the pile of ash that had recently been his friend. All traces of lust were gone from his eyes. Now he looked positively murderous.

"Are you a magic wielder?" he spat.

So that *was* a thing here.

"Release me," I repeated.

Keeping one hand on my waist, Knut reached down to scoop up my dagger. "Give me one reason I shouldn't kill you where you stand."

"If you kill me, Clan Ragnar will wage a war upon your tribe unlike anything you've ever seen," I lied. "Your insolence already cost Markus his life. Are you so ready to seal the fate of your chief?"

Hatred spewed from Knut's eyes as he shoved my dagger into his belt and pulled a length of rope from his pouch. He forced my wrists in front of my waist and tied them together. Then he pulled the axe from his back and shoved me forward.

"Walk. Chief Olav will decide your fate. And if he casts you out . . ." Knut stepped closer, wrapping his fingers around my curls in a rough yank, ". . . you're mine."

I shoved my fear deep down, wrenched my head from his grasp, and marched determinedly forward. I hoped the Viking mistook my silence for strength.

How in the hell was I going to get out of this?

CHAPTER 3

THE BEACH WAS MUCH closer than I would have liked. During our too-short march, I prayed for a distraction—anything to pull Knut's attention away just long enough for me to make a run for it. Though what I'd do with myself surrounded by a bear-infested forest in a magic-infused era, I did not know.

Back in the village, the pungent tang of blood filled the beach, where partially maimed Vikings laid in varying states of injury and death. My gut churned, bile rising in my throat. I turned my head from the carpet of carcasses and studied the settlement. There were roughly fifty wooden structures there, along with a pasture and multiple crop fields. From the little I knew about Viking life—most of which had come from Mormor's stories and summer trips to the Norwegian History Museum—I gathered this was one of the bigger settlements. Which meant this was one of the bigger, and therefore more violent, tribes.

I was totally screwed.

Not screwed, Saga. Challenged. We are only given the challenges that we have the strength to overcome.

Positive thinking had better work in whatever year this was.

"Walk faster." Cold metal pressed into my back as Knut pushed me forward.

I stumbled, then pulled my roped wrists apart and lifted the hem of my skirt a few inches before continuing on. As I moved, I subtly scanned my surroundings, cataloguing buildings—and sentries—for whenever I had an opportunity to escape. Most of the wooden structures were small, single-story huts set a few hundred yards back from the beach. They had green, thatched roofs and simple front doors. But as we moved farther from the ocean, the structures grew larger and the doors more ornate. A pasture led off a two-story building that must have been a barn, and within the fence roamed sheep, pigs, and a handful of farmhands. The men paid me no mind, but the women looked up curiously, mud coating their skirts and hands. Their eyes flickered from my raised chin to my bound wrists, their faces settling into masks of . . . was that pity?

Panic later, Saga. Collect information now.

Right.

Knut shoved me again as I marched past a small hut. A comforting scent wafted through the open door, where I glimpsed a barefooted woman turning something that looked an awful lot like lefse—the same Norwegian flatbread I baked with my grandmother. I walked farther, past women emerging from the mid-sized wooden huts. They carried buckets, bandages, and cloths as they ran to the beach. They were probably heading down to care for the wounded . . . and cover the deceased.

"Looks like your surviving clansmen have made a sizeable donation to our thrall pool." Knut laughed. "I wonder if Chief Olav will decide to make an example out of the new slaves. We haven't made a sacrifice in a while."

"You sacrifice humans?" I blurted. What nightmare world had that God-forsaken dagger delivered me to?

Knut's lips curled up in a cruel smile. I clamped my jaw shut.

"It's a shame the rest of the tribes never embraced the practice. But then, they always were soft . . . which will make our negotiations at the *Ting* much easier."

A thousand questions competed for dominance in my brain, ranging from *what's the Ting* to *how do I stay off the human-sacrifice list*? But before I could voice any of them, Knut shoved me to my left.

"Chief Olav lives up here."

I raised my chin and marched forward, ignoring the curious stares of the women outside the larger houses. They wore flowing blouses and dresses equal in length to mine, all in varying shades of green. Some had elaborate embroidery on the hems, while others were embellished with silver clasps and beltloops. They all bore expressions identical to the farmers'—compassion. Sadness. Pity.

For me.

When we reached the largest hut, Knut shoved me down. I held back my cry as my knees cracked atop a rock. The brute shoved me again, and my fists pounded into the ground. The action sent mud splattering up the front of my dress. A thick drop landed on my cheek.

"*Hei!*" Knut bellowed. "Chief Olav, I have a captive for you!"

The hut's intricately carved wooden door flew open, revealing a man who must have descended from giants. His shoulders stretched from one side of the doorframe to the other, and he had to duck as he stepped out onto the wooden step. Wild, red hair sprouted from every spot on his face, from his thick, bushy brows, to his frizzy, braided beard. He cracked his knuckles menacingly, making his sinewy biceps flex against his matted, fur vest. If the blood covering his torso was any indication, he'd just finished slaying my so-called clansmen on the beach.

Gulp.

"What have you done with her?" the chief growled. "She's filthy."

I reached up with bound wrists and wiped the mud from my face.

"Nothing, I swear." Knut raised his right hand. "I

22

wouldn't break your command. Not before your son chooses his bride. But once he does . . . assuming he doesn't choose this female . . ."

I shot Knut a glare packed with so much heat, I was surprised he didn't incinerate on the spot.

Olav chuckled. "Why would Lars choose a thrall? I shall select a free female for him; perhaps the daughter of a rival clan, one who can strengthen our alliances and expand our trade routes."

Oh, God.

"Then this female should be of great interest to you. She's not a slave." Knut raised my dagger in his hands. "She's Clan Ragnar."

Fear threatened to choke me as Olav's brows furrowed. A low growl built in his chest, and I knew Knut had just sealed my fate. I also knew I might never get a better chance to escape. If I didn't grab the dagger and make a run for it, I'd be trapped in this human-sacrificing world for God knew how long.

Just do it. Now.

I drew a breath, tugged against my bindings, and lunged for the dagger. My palms wrapped around the hilt and I swung wildly, forcing Knut to the ground with an errant jab as I turned for the forest. My toes dug into the mud while I pumped my legs and ran away from Olav's house.

Much too soon, cold fingers wrapped around my neck. I was wrenched upward in one painful move-ment. My hands flew to my throat, and I pushed the dagger toward the massive hand that blocked my breath, while my feet flailed at my captor.

"She's a spirited one." Olav swung his arm to the side and stared at me. The world wavered as oxygen deprivation settled in. I jabbed my blade at Olav's arm, but he ripped the dagger from my hand before I could cause any damage.

"Can't," I gasped, "breathe."

"I could do far worse to you," Olav whispered before turning to Knut. "How do you know she's from Clan Ragnar?"

"She says she's one of theirs. And I found *that* with her." Knut pointed at the dagger.

"That *is* interesting." Olav set me on my feet, holding tight to my upper arm as he studied the weapon. I leaned into his weight, spots swimming before my eyes.

Escape plan fail.

"I'll see to it that Ragnar's heir is . . . looked after. I'd been intending to forge an alliance with Clan Ankor, but Clan Ragnar's fealty would be considerably more favorable."

"She may wield magic," Knut warned. "Markus died in possession of that dagger."

Olav's hand tightened around my arm. "Is that true?"

"I . . ." I had no idea how to play the magic card. It hadn't scared Knut enough to free me. And if these people were anti-magic, it might get me burned at the stake—or whatever Vikings did to witches. Not wanting to tip my hand, I pulled my shoulders back and avoided the question. "Clan Ragnar will slaughter all of you if you don't return me home, unharmed."

Olav's soulless laugh chilled my heart. "Your tribe doesn't have our numbers. And they certainly don't have our bloodlust. We just massacred half of your warriors. Who will save you now?"

It would have been a stellar time for the dagger to incinerate someone. Anyone. But it did nothing while Olav dragged me through the mud, and across the village. When he reached one of the smaller huts, he flung open the door and shoved me inside. I stumbled over an uneven floorboard, tripping and landing hard on my already-bruised hip. *Ow!*

"You'll stay in one of our slave huts with two other thralls until my son returns from his raid." Olav shoved my dagger into his belt and turned to Knut. "You'll make sure she doesn't escape. And you won't lay a finger on my son's bride. Are we clear?"

Knut's eyes narrowed, but he lowered his head in submission. "*Ja*," he vowed.

Olav leaned through the door. "If you use so much as a whisper of magic while you're in here, it's straight to the altar for sacrifice. Do *you* understand?"

I jutted my jaw, refusing to answer.

"Don't test me," Olav warned. "You won't like the way our tribe punishes women."

Olav slammed the door in my face, his footsteps like cannon fire as he stormed away.

Alone in the windowless hut, I pulled my knees to

my chest, drew a shaky breath, and allowed myself a moment of vulnerability.

It was the only time I permitted myself to cry.

CHAPTER 4

THE TWO WEEKS THAT FOLLOWED were the most disconcerting of my life. My first day of college had come and gone, and I hadn't been there to experience it. My heart ached for my family—especially the grandmother who'd raised me, and the cousin who should have been my dorm-mate. While in my new reality . . .

Through Clan Bjorn's slaves I learned that women in this world were considered chattel—property to be managed as their male overlords saw fit. Wives maintained the home and oversaw the grunt work associated with their husband's profession—farmers' wives mucked the stables, warriors' wives cleaned blood from battle gear, and the clan leaders' wives were granted the privilege of weaving garments until their fingers practically bled. While slaves . . . *God.* Slaves' lives were literally hell on earth. I couldn't fathom how the girls I'd met had survived for so long.

I shared my hut with two girls who were no more than eighteen years old. Ingrid was a feisty redhead with sparkling green eyes and a smattering of freckles across her cherubic cheeks. She'd arrived six months ago as a tribute offered in exchange for Clan Bjorn's protection. Her eyes had not yet lost their defiant spark. And though she tilled the crops from dawn until dusk, she returned each night full of hope that one day she would escape Clan Bjorn . . . and exact revenge on the family who'd sentenced her to a life of misery.

Vidia was a raven-haired girl whose coffee-colored eyes lacked any sign of light. She was soft-spoken, with an air of sorrow that haunted her listless gait as she shuffled through the door each night. Her job was to assist the clan butcher, and she returned to our hut every day covered in animal blood. One night she didn't return at all, and I worried that she'd been hurt. But she crept through the door in the early morning hours, crawling atop the single straw mat that served as a bed for the three of us, and cried herself to sleep.

I didn't want to think about what she'd been through.

One evening, both girls arrived home before sundown and plopped onto our bed, exhausted. I took the opportunity to ask them about our captors. Ingrid played with the ends of her braids as she explained Clan Bjorn was one of the fiercest tribes in Scandinavia, second only to a tribe called Valkyris. Though inter-tribal accords prohibited clans from attacking allies, our captors regularly raided local villages and sent their most heartless warriors on voyages overseas. Their reputation as murderous pillagers extended throughout Europe, and the riches they'd acquired—along with the threat they imposed—allowed them to purchase members of allied tribes as slaves. This ensured Clan Bjorn was rarely threatened, as tribes were reluctant to not only start a battle they'd likely lose, but to attack the group who owned their kin.

"Everything about them sounds awful." I tucked my knees up to my chest. "Are all the tribes like this?"

"Most in this region are," Vidia's quiet voice confirmed. "There's rumor of a tribe where women are respected—given the same rights and responsibilities as men. The story goes that their society is ruled by a male *and* female chief, and their children are allowed to choose their vocation regardless of their parents' trade."

"I've heard that story!" Ingrid sat up with a frown. "I wish it was true."

"It's not?" I asked.

"No." Vidia sighed. "Nobody has ever been to their village—or met anyone from their clan. It's a nice idea, but it's no more than a legend—something mothers tell to their children at bedtime."

"I wish it was real, though." Ingrid leaned forward. "I'd love to be a warrior. I'd slaughter every last monster who intimidated women, and children, and . . . well, anyone!"

I made a mental note not to get on Ingrid's bad side. And to sleep with one eye open if I did.

"Some tribes allow women to fight, though," Vidia added. "I've never seen them, but I've heard shield-maidens are every bit as terrifying as their male counterparts."

"Imagine an all-female army descending on Clan Bjorn." Ingrid closed her eyes with a sanguine smile. "They'd free us from this Helheim, and welcome us into their tribe."

"Keep dreaming, Ingrid." Vidia offered a sad smile. "It's better than living in this world."

"You said there was another tribe that's worse than this one," I hedged. "The . . . Valkia?"

"Valkyris," Ingrid confirmed. "And they're *truly* terrifying. The fiercest, most forceful tribe in the northern countries. Clans do *not* get on their bad side —if they do, they awake to discover their entire village burned right to the ground."

"If they awake at all." Vidia shuddered. "The Valkyris don't take slaves—they just murder captives on the spot. My brother once witnessed one of their raids. He was scouting the coast for a farm site when Valkyris ships appeared on the horizon. There was a village nearby—one that must have done something to upset the Valkyris. Not only did they slaughter most of the villagers, but their dragons came in afterward and burned the entire area down. By the time they left, the village was nothing but ash."

My jaw landed on my chest. "There are *dragons* here?"

"They live where the Valkyris do." Ingrid shrugged.

"But nobody knows where they keep their camp. If that ever got out, there would be a massive raid, for sure."

Right.

I changed tack. "What do you know about Clan Bjorn's heir? Lars?"

Vidia cringed. "He's a monster. Stay as far from him as you can."

"I don't think that's going to be an option." I pushed at my cuticles. "Apparently, I'm supposed to marry him."

"No!" Ingrid's eyes widened. "You can't do that. He's awful."

My shoulders drooped. A tiny part of me had thought maybe the girls would say Lars was the one decent guy in the tribe—that this forced marriage wouldn't be as bad as it sounded.

That's what thought got you, Saga.

Vidia placed a hand atop my knee. "Lars intends to run the tribe as his father has—raiding, pillaging, and expanding his circle of influence at the expense of neighboring clans. He's said that once he assumes leadership, Clan Bjorn will grow its army until *this* is the most feared tribe in the land."

"Great." I sighed. "So basically, the rest of my life is going to suck."

The girls tilted their heads in confusion.

"It's going to be, uh . . ." How had Ingrid put it? "It'll be Helheim."

My hut-mates nodded.

"I'm so sorry, Saga," Vidia whispered.

"It's fine." I forced a smile. "Maybe he won't even like me—from what I understand, Lars can reject me, and then Olav will have to use me as a kind of a bargaining chip at something called the *Ting*."

"The *Ting* is just days away." Vidia frowned. "And Lars still hasn't returned from his raid. What will Olav do if he isn't home in time?"

"No clue." I sighed. "But that's tomorrow's problem. Right now, I'm just wondering how I'm going to get any sleep with Ingrid snoring in my ear."

"I do not snore!" Ingrid swatted me.

"You do," Vidia confirmed.

Ingrid crossed her arms.

"But we don't mind. I'm just happy you're finally sleeping peacefully." Vidia turned to me. "When Ingrid first arrived, she had nightmares so terrible, she woke half the tribe with her screams. The beatings they put her through for it were horrendous."

Fire flashed in Ingrid's eyes. "You have to escape this place, Saga. Maybe when you're at the *Ting*, they'll leave you unguarded long enough to—"

"Don't give her hope," Vidia said softly. "Just pray that one day, the gods extract revenge on this tribe. Maybe then, we'll finally be free."

My heart sunk as I looked at the two girls—one defeated and desolate, the other fiery and fierce. They deserved so much more than the life they'd been forced into.

I would find some way to give it to them. Even if I had no idea how.

❄

The morning of the *Ting* dawned crisp, cool and clear. I'd barely managed to open my eyes before I was marched to the ocean by two of Olav's personal maids, who put me through a thorough cleansing. The maids then led me back to my hut, where I was groomed to within an inch of my life. Ingrid wove my hair into an intricate crown of braids, and Vidia helped me into an elaborate blue gown. Scouts had spotted Lars' boats returning from the raid, and I was to look my best for him. If I was deemed pleasing enough, I would join him at the *Ting*, where we would lord our betrothal over my so-called clan. If I wasn't, well . . . Ingrid was confident Clan Ragnar would barter for my return.

"Try not to worry, Saga." Ingrid tucked the final braid against my scalp. "They're your family. I'm sure they'll pay whatever ransom Lars asks for."

I didn't have the heart to tell her the truth—nobody from Clan Ragnar would have a clue who I was. And I had no idea how I was going to survive explaining that to a tribe who still practiced human sacrifice.

Human. Freaking. Sacrifice.

I wrung my hands together, wondering for the hundredth time in the past two weeks how I was going to get myself out of all this, when shouts from the beach pulled me from my thoughts.

"They're home! Everybody, to the beach!"

Vidia poked her head out of the door, then looked back with a nod. "It's them."

Ingrid squeezed my hand in hers. "Are you ready?"

"No," I said honestly. "Not even close."

"He's not unattractive," Ingrid offered.

"But he is unkind," Vidia said quietly. "I hope you escape."

"So do I," I whispered.

Vidia reached over to clasp my other hand. She, Ingrid, and I stood in silence until Olav's fierce bellow pierced the calm.

"Get out here and greet my son!"

I drew my shoulders back, released my friends' hands, and marched into the light. Ingrid and Vidia fell in step beside me as I followed a glaring Olav to the beach, where three long, wooden ships were moored in the water. Their sailors waded through the surf, arms laden with treasure as they made their way to the shore.

"Which is Lars?" I murmured from the corner of my mouth.

"The one at the water's edge, dragging two new thralls," Vidia whispered back.

I scanned the shore until I spotted a tall man with long, crimson hair and thick, sinewy shoulders. Olav's younger doppelganger yanked on a rope, and two girls who were no older than me lurched forward. Their hands were tied together, just as mine had been not long ago, and they stumbled as their captor wrenched them through the surf.

"He's awful," I whispered.

"I know," Vidia whispered back.

Despair pooled in my heart. Despite my new friends' assertions, a tiny part of me had held out hope that Lars might be my saving grace—a decent soul who was as disgusted by his tribe's barbaric practices as I was. But if the way he treated those girls was any indication, he was as brutish as his father and clansmen.

And I was supposed to marry him.

Okay, Saga. Here we go.

Lars handed the slaves to Knut, and I turned to Ingrid. "Promise me whatever happens today, you'll do everything you can to keep that monster away from those girls. Help them get out of here, and you along with them."

"How?" Ingrid whispered.

"I don't know . . ." I worried my bottom lip. "Listen, there should be a bear carcass with some arrows in its neck about five minutes into the forest. Try to fake a distraction and get to it—one of the sheep could go missing, or a goat could get lost, I don't know. Just head north from the barn and you'll find it. Extract the arrows, and if you can get your hands on a bow . . ."

I drew my shoulders back and mimicked the movement of shooting an arrow. All those years of archery training were about to come in handy. "Keep your fingers light and aim low—beginners tend to pull up on release, which raises the impact-line."

"Saga." Vidia frowned. "Nobody's ever escaped Clan Bjorn."

"Maybe not yet," I agreed. "But the impossible always takes a bit longer. Right?"

A slow smile slid across Ingrid's face. She clasped my hand. "Good luck, Saga."

"Good luck to *you*." I squeezed her hand.

My gaze slid to the beach, where Lars stormed up the rocks. His wet shirt clung to his chest as he pulled his sword from its sheath and dropped to one knee before Olav.

"My chief." Lars' gravelly voice was steady as he lowered his head.

"My son," Olav returned. "Rise, and meet your bride."

Lars' eyes flicked upward, annoyance thick within their rich, green depths. "And which clan has produced the highest bid? Was it Ankor?"

"Ragnar," Olav purred. "They sent an heir with their recent attack party."

Lars stood slowly. His eyes roved between Vidia and Ingrid before finally settling on me. He barely glanced at my golden braids and freshly made-up face before shifting his gaze down my dress; its wide neck revealed an expanse of skin from my shoulders to my chest, and Lars spent enough time sizing up my cleavage that I strongly considered slapping him.

Time and place, Saga. Get the dagger back first.

Right.

"She'll do," Lars drawled.

"Excellent." Olav nodded. "We shall arrange the

wedding festivities after we have secured Clan Ragnar's fealty."

"I trust my marriage will expand our territory?" Lars' gaze roamed down my body, settling somewhere intimate.

Time. Place. No slapping.

Ugh.

"It will. And it will secure our future," Olav added. "Your bride might well be a magic wielder. Once she's a member of Clan Bjorn, she will be bound to use her talents to protect our tribe."

"Not to destroy it." Lars *finally* met my eyes. "Father, you have outdone yourself. You've extended our raid routes and given us a tactical advantage in one . . ." his eyes returned to my cleavage, ". . . *exquisite* package."

I folded my arms across my chest. "And if I refuse to marry you?"

Laughter rumbled in Lars' throat. "Why, Father. You've gifted me a fighter. How delightful."

Olav's brow furrowed. "Punish her, boy."

"Oh, I will." Lars twirled his sword lightly. "I intend to extract a great deal of enjoyment from you, heir of Ragnar."

A shudder wracked my spine, but I forced myself to stay still. I wouldn't give Lars the satisfaction of knowing how deeply he frightened me. I had to find a way to escape this marriage.

The *Ting* was my very last hope.

"I'm not your female," I spat.

"Ah, but you are," he said. "And women in my tribe have no rights. Too bad the rest of the clans haven't come around to our line of thought."

God, these men had to be stopped.

"*Velkommen,* Clan Bjorn!"

The call pulled me from my worries. I stared into the distance to find several men at the edge of a circle of boulders. There were nine rocks in total, each standing almost four feet tall.

Hold on. I knew this place. It was the Iron Age graveyard near Mormor's cabin. My cousins and I had visited it as kids. We'd played hide-and-seek among the stones until Uncle Jon told us it had once been a sacred, Viking meeting spot—one where chiefs and their heirs came to discuss inter-tribal politics, and rule on matters that affected the greater Scandinavian world. He'd told me it was the site of the Thing.

Oh. The Thing. Ting. Right.

"Someone's arrived early." Lars removed his hand from my waist and pulled his horse alongside Olav's. "I thought only tribal leaders were scheduled to meet today."

"The weather must have been favorable. Several groups are already here." Olav nudged his horse to a trot. "And it looks as if they've brought their travel parties with them."

There went my grab-the-dagger-and-run-before-anyone-saw-me plan.

Lars kicked his horse with a mighty cry. He

matched Olav's pace, and before I knew it, we'd reached the circle of rocks. Lars pulled me from his mount, and tied the animal to a nearby tree before binding my wrists together and dragging me to the largest of the rocks. I glared at his back, taking a small amount of satisfaction in the way he leaned slightly to the right as he walked. My elbow had been well aimed. Served him right.

Olav took his place beside us, and raised his hand in greeting. "*Velkommen,*" he boomed.

Seven chiefs and their heirs stepped into the circle. "*Velkommen.*"

"Apologies for our delayed arrival—my son has only just returned from raiding a northern settlement." Olav nodded to Lars, who rested one hand menacingly atop his sword. "Chieftains, as is this hosting tribe's tradition, today's session will be reserved for our personal matters. Inform your travel parties they may return to present their business in the morning."

A brief moment of chaos ensued, in which the chiefs and their heirs took their places in the circle, while representatives of the travel parties directed their members into the forest behind the stones. From what Ingrid had told me about this event, I knew there were campsites, cooking pits, and gallons of ale nestled within those evergreens. My eyes darted to my dagger, still resting securely against Olav's hip. The second I got my hands on it, I'd run straight for the camp—no doubt I could lose myself in the sea of Norsemen, and then . . .

And then what? Where would I go? How would I protect myself? These woods were chock-full of Vikings I could see, and hungry animals I couldn't. And despite its initial Markus-melting performance, the dagger didn't seem particularly keen on helping me out.

That's Afternoon Saga's problem. Morning Saga just needs to escape. One problem at a time, remember?

"We appear to be missing a chieftain," Olav bellowed.

"Chief Halvar is on his way," called a brown-haired man. His position between one of the rocks and a more sizeable, younger version of himself confirmed his status as chief of a tribe. I wondered if his people practiced human sacrifice.

Shudder.

"Chief Halvar," Olav spat. "That man repeatedly disrespects our customs. His insolence undermines our traditions. It should be cause to eject Clan Valkyris from the alliance of Western Tri—"

"Now, Olav. No need to stage an uprising. We're right here." The smooth voice came from the slope behind me. I turned until I locked eyes with a blond-haired, sword-wielding man atop a grey horse. The corners of his mouth angled downward as he scanned the set of my jaw, the ropes at my wrist, and the way Lars' knuckles whitened as he pulled me closer. The man shook his head before nudging his horse forward. He trotted to the base of the knoll, tied his animal to a

41

low-hanging tree branch, and took his place at the last empty stone.

"You may proceed." Halvar nodded.

"You said *we're* here," Olav said through gritted teeth. "Am I to presume your heir is running even later than you are?"

"Oh, no. He will arrive . . ." Halvar closed his eyes and drew a slow breath. "Now."

"The old man still thinks he's a magic wielder," Lars hissed.

"My son was dealing with an insurgent. One of yours, I believe, Olav. That will be one less in your travel party on the trip home." Halvar opened his eyes, and held a hand toward the knoll. "*Velkommen,* Erik. I trust you've handled the problem?"

"I have." The menacing voice from the top of the hill sent icicles snaking through my vertebrae. I turned again, this time taking in the massive blond-maned Viking atop an enormous black horse. Broad shoulders tugged against his vest, revealing arms so muscular they could have been lifted straight from a superhero movie. He nudged his horse forward, the ensuing canter sending unruly blond hair streaming behind him. All the while his biceps remained flexed, as if he were preparing for a fight. From the way he glowered at Lars, I had no doubt who his first target would be.

Gulp.

"You injured one of our men?" Olav barked.

"I killed the one who shot an arrow at my back." Muscles swung his leg over his horse, his shoulders tensing as he tied the animal to the same tree as his father's. "Still no honor among your tribe?"

Olav bristled. "Your insolence will cost you."

One corner of Erik's mouth turned up in an easy smirk. "Our wealth runs deeper than yours, Olav. But then, you already know that."

Lars' fingers tightened around my wrists, the pain intensifying until I could no longer stifle my yelp.

"Silence!" Lars wrenched my arms so suddenly that I stumbled. The movement caught Muscles' attention, and he froze on the way to his stone. His clear, blue eyes held mine for an endless moment, during which my heart thundered and my head spun. God, those eyes were spectacular. They studied me with unbridled curiosity, a brief flicker of sympathy passing across their bottomless, azure depths before shuttering closed. When they opened, Muscles' sympathy was gone. A callous coldness had settled into its place.

"What do you have there, Lars?" Boredom laced Muscles' tone. "New plaything?"

"*Ja*," Lars drawled. "One that previously belonged to Clan Ragnar, if I'm not mistaken."

Oh, *skit. Skit, skit, skit.* This was it. I was about to be outed.

Grab the dagger and run, Saga. Now. Do it!

Panic coursed through my veins, leaving icy trails along my insides. Before I could chicken out, I bent my knees and ripped my arms from Lars' grip. The movement caught him off balance, and as he stepped backward I swung my leg in a low arc, kicking his foot out from under him. He landed on his butt in the grass, but I knew he wouldn't stay down for long. With Olav seemingly distracted by the string of curses streaming from his son, I seized the opportunity and lunged for the dagger. My palms wrapped around the hilt and I tore it from Olav's belt, then bolted for the forest. As I ran, I prayed for a miracle.

"Okay, dagger. Activate." My feet pounded the grass as I sprinted away from the brutes. "I said, activate! Take me home! Go!"

When nothing happened, I slapped the face of the dagger against my palm. "Magic, on! Arugh! Come on, *please!*"

Thunderous steps stampeded behind me. The too-close shouts of angry Vikings filled my heart with fear, but I channeled the energy into my muscles and ran harder. I had one shot at escape. If I failed—and if they didn't kill me—I knew I'd never get my hands on the dagger again.

This was my one chance to go home.

"Work. Please! Take me back to my own time before —oh, God!" A scream ripped from my throat as thick hands circled my neck and lifted me into the air. I swung wildly at my assailant, my dagger making fierce swipes at whichever monster had managed to catch me. Whoever it was loosened his grip just enough that I wouldn't choke, and I sucked in a long draw before driving the point of my dagger into the arm that held me. A curse ripped from my attacker's lips as he tore the dagger from his arm. I clawed frantically at the

CHAPTER 5

T HE RIDE TO THE *Ting* was interminable. The attending members of Clan Bjorn rode or walked a respectable distance behind Olav and his son. Lars had insisted I join him on his horse, and he pressed himself firmly against my back for the entire duration of the ten-mile ride. Olav kept my dagger at his waist—he said he planned to return it to Clan Ragnar as part of the fealty bribe. But that dagger was the key to my getting back home—I hoped—and I fully intended to rip it from his belt and run for the hills before my supposed-family could out me as a stranger.

I just had to pray an opportunity presented itself.

As we neared the *Ting*, Lars' hold on my waist shifted slowly upward. I delivered a swift elbow to his ribcage, eliciting a menacing chuckle that rumbled against my back.

"Very good, Heir Ragnar." His breath was hot against my ear. "I like my females feisty."

blood-covered hilt, but the brute pulled it away from me before setting me lightly on the ground. Warm breath tickled my ear as he leaned forward and whispered, "Say nothing. Just trust me."

What?

I kicked backward, hoping to strike his shins. But the Viking stepped easily to my side, wrapping one massive arm around me and locking me in place. I stood, shoulders squared to the forest, silently willing the dagger to do what I couldn't.

Please, please just help me escape.

The forest was fifty feet away. The revelers were just beyond that. I'd been so close.

And I'd failed.

My head dropped, my chin quivering as I fought against tears I would not shed. Not today.

I wouldn't let them see me cry.

"Hand her over." Lars' hateful voice rang through the air. When I cringed, the arm around my shoulder tensed.

"She's mine now." My captor spun me around. I took in Lars' furious glare, Olav's white-knuckled grip on his sword, and the horde of angry chieftains and heirs circled behind them. None of the Vikings looked familiar, which meant I had just become the unwitting property of . . .

"Erik. Hand. Her. Over." Lars spoke through gritted teeth.

"I don't make the laws." Erik's shoulder lifted, as if in a shrug. "I just enforce them."

Lars stepped forward, his hand on the hilt of his sword. "Last chance. Release her, or Valkyris will find itself lacking an heir."

Valkyris. I was in the possession of the only tribe more feared than Bjorn. *Skit.*

Olav positioned himself directly beside his son. He slowly drew his own sword.

Erik angled me behind him, holding my arm with one hand so I was shielded by his massive torso. "Threaten me again and your clan will find itself lacking in *all* leadership."

Lars bristled, hatred darkening his eyes. My hands trembled as I realized how close I was to two Vikings who, from all appearances, were about to kill each other. Muscles was a big guy, but there was only so much protection a single body could afford.

Even an impressively built, exceedingly firm, deliciously leather-clad one.

I willed my dagger to help me find a way out of this. But it remained firmly in Erik's blood-soaked hand, emitting absolutely no magic. And Erik's hold on my arm offered absolutely no give.

Skit.

Olav placed a hand atop his son's shoulder before turning to Erik. "What terms do you offer?"

"Terms?" Erik laughed, a cold, emotionless bark that resonated through the meadow. "The moment she left your control, she ceased to belong to you. There will be no terms."

Lars' arm twitched, and Halvar moved to stand beside his son.

"Careful, Lars," Halvar warned. "I've promised our dragons a raid, and I'd hate for them to *accidentally* come upon an allied camp."

So, Vidia had been right about the dragons. Good God, did they all have dragons? *Breathe, Saga. Breathe.*

"You wouldn't dare," Olav hissed.

"You know, I've never actually seen your dragons. I'm starting to wonder if they even exist," Lars growled.

Okay, so they didn't *all* have dragons. Just the ones who'd taken me hostage.

Not better.

"I'd be more than happy to arrange a face-to-face," Erik said coolly.

"Silence!" Olav barked. "We will release our claim on the girl in exchange for another three years' protection. No raids on our tribe, human or otherwise."

"One year," Halvar said calmly. "You'll receive the same terms as the rest of our allies."

Lars looked like he wanted to rip Halvar's head from his neck, but Olav's white-knuckled grip seemed to keep him firmly in place.

"We accept your terms." Olav holstered his sword. "This girl cost me one of my warriors. Clan Ragnar must be glad to be rid of her."

Oh, God.

My stomach plummeted as one of the chiefs tilted his head. "I don't understand what you—"

"Erik," Halvar interrupted loudly. "Take your prize

back to our fortress. I'll follow once I conclude our dealings here."

The blonde's camp had a fortress? How the hell was I going to break out of *that*?

"No respect for tradition," Olav grunted. "The celebrations won't be over for at least a week."

"We have no pending legal matters," Halvar said. "And our dragons are hungry."

Nobody argued with him.

The chiefs and the heirs made their way back to the stones, Lars shooting lethal glares over his shoulder the entire way. Once they'd taken their positions and continued with their dialogue, Erik tucked my dagger into his belt. Since my hands were still bound, he used the rope to lead me to his horse. He easily lifted me onto its shoulders before climbing up after me, his thick thighs straining against tight leather pants.

No, Saga. Do not watch his muscles. Make a move for the dagger!

"Don't bother trying to get the dagger," Erik said calmly. I blinked back at him as he nudged his horse into an easy walk. "And try not to give away your next move by staring. If you hadn't noticed, I'm the least of your worries."

"Yeah. Right," I muttered. I turned around, gripping the horse's mane as Erik rode over the grassy knoll, past the forest where the clans had set up their tents, and into a vast expanse of rolling, green fields. When we neared a stream, he slid his palm across my stomach and pressed me against him.

My elbow struck swiftly. "Don't get any ideas. I wasn't having it with the last guy who pulled that move, and I'm not about to let you try."

Amusement colored Erik's tone. "Unless you want to be thrown from a horse, I suggest you choose your battles more wisely."

"How dare you—oh!" My heart jumped into my throat as the horse launched itself over the stream. I flailed backward, begrudgingly grateful for Erik's firm grip. "Fine, I'll let you . . . stabilize me, then."

Erik tightened his grip around my waist. With a shout, he pushed his horse into a gallop. My butt bounced wildly as I struggled to find the rhythm of the animal's gait. I'd ridden one horse, once . . . and then I'd had a saddle and reins. Riding bareback with nothing but an enormous Viking to save me from an equine-induced death was a challenge for which I was not prepared.

And one I'd have very much liked to decline.

We rode for what felt like forever, crossing fields and jumping rivers before Erik finally slowed his horse to a trot. He led the animal to a stream, and slid from its back. I scooted toward its rear as it lowered its head to drink.

"Do I get down too?" I asked.

Erik shrugged. "If you're thirsty. And don't bother running—I'll only catch you again."

I waited until Erik bent down to scoop water from the river before I glared at his back. He may have been a dragon-owning, fortress-dwelling Viking heir, but he was also a jerk.

One day, I'd tell him to his face.

For now, I slid my bound wrists across the horse's belly and tried to swing my leg over its back. Maybe if I leaned forward, I could . . .

"Arugh!" I lost my grip.

Erik looked up from the river as I tumbled ungracefully to the ground. Amusement danced in his clear, blue eyes as he called up, "You okay?"

"I've been better," I muttered. Pushing an errant braid off my face, I climbed to my feet and stomped to the river. "So, how do we do this?"

"How do we do what? Drink?" Erik raised a brow. "Tell me I didn't just risk a blood feud for a girl whose skill set doesn't include water consumption?"

"For your information, I've never drinken— drunken—drinked—" I rolled my eyes. "I've never had water from a stream before."

Erik tilted his head. "Where do you get your water from?"

The tap. The filter. Little glass bottles that originated near a Norwegian lake.

"Uh, the usual places." I waved my hand in the air.

"Mmm." Erik cupped his hands together and dipped them into the stream before raising them to his mouth. "Hurry up. I want to reach the halfway point before dark."

The halfway point? Jeez, how far away was this fortress? And how was I going to find my way back to

Mormor's cabin from whatever corner of the world—and decade in time—concealed it?

We rode the rest of the way in silence. A million questions danced through my mind, but I kept them to myself as we made our way down a steep, windy trail, raced along the edge of a fjord, and began the long trek up a waterfall-lined mountain. When the trees thickened and a light snow dusted the ground, Erik slid off the horse and led it into the woods on foot.

"Do I get down too, or—"

"No."

Well, fine.

We walked for another five minutes, until the trees thinned and the whoosh of rushing water broke the silence. Erik turned left at a massive boulder, pulling his horse forward until he reached a small log cabin. It stood near the edge of the waterfall, set back just enough that the spray didn't reach its grass-lined roof. It had a tidy front porch, a small stable, and a neat pile of wood stacked outside the ornately carved door. It would have been absolutely charming . . . if it weren't the latest in a series of places I'd be trying to escape.

Erik reached up to help me off the horse. "Didn't want to see you take another tumble."

I bit back my retort.

"We'll spend the night here," Erik said. "And be in Valkyris by early evening."

"Great."

Erik raised one blond brow. "I meant what I said

about running. Our dragons patrol the area by air, so it's to your benefit to stay in the *huset*."

Holy *skit*. Was he serious?

I waited on the porch as Erik led his horse to the stable. He returned, dusting hay off his arms before pushing open the sturdy, front door. Nerves danced in my abdomen as he held out a hand and waited for me to step across the threshold.

I assessed my situation. On the one hand, I was alone in the woods with a massive Viking—the most heartless member of the most fear-inducing tribe in the entire region. But on the other hand, Erik hadn't laid a finger on me . . . yet. Even though I'd stabbed him, insulted him, and made no attempt to hide my disgust at his very existence, he didn't seem inclined to retaliate.

Unless he was waiting for just the right moment.

Like the moment I fell asleep.

Oh, God. Don't sleep. Run.

No. Don't run. Dragons.

I'm so screwed.

I glanced up at Erik, willing the fear to ebb from my eyes. He raised a brow and gestured toward the entry. "Well?"

Right. I summoned a strength I didn't feel as I drew a deep breath, pulled my shoulders back, and stepped into the cabin.

And I prayed I hadn't made a huge mistake.

CHAPTER 6

"THERE'S ONLY ONE BED!" I whirled on Erik as the door clicked behind me. "I wasn't kidding, buddy. If you think anything's going to happen here"—I waved my fingers between the two of us—"then you've got another thing coming."

"Ouch." Erik's boots clicked against the wooden floorboards as he moved into the cabin. The space was so tiny, and his legs were so long, he reached the far wall in mere steps. Once there, he bent down and transferred logs into the stone fireplace. When orange flames lapped at the hearth, he turned to me with an expectant stare.

"What?" I asked.

"I could use some more wood."

And I could use a one-way ticket home. "And?"

Erik looked at me as if I'd caught the stupid. "And . . . it is on the front porch."

I glared. "That's right. Since I'm your property now, I'm supposed to serve you."

"You don't serve anyone." Erik crossed the room, marched through the front door, and returned carrying an armful of logs. "But some help would be nice."

Oh. Right.

"My wrists are still bound," I said quietly.

Erik deposited the firewood before returning to me. My eye-level hit at the middle of his chest, and when I looked up, sky-blue eyes studied me curiously. My captor ran one hand through his tangle of shoulder-length hair before exhaling slowly. With surprising gentleness, he took my hands in his and turned them over. A surge of heat shot from his rough fingers up my arm. My breathing quickened, and I hastily broke our eye contact.

Holy mother.

Calloused fingers traced light circles in my palm, sending a fresh wave of heat—this one extending all the way down my legs. My knees buckled, and Erik quickly placed a hand on my waist.

"Are you feeling all right?"

"Mmm-hmm." *Focus, Saga. Feel nothing. Even if he is ridiculously hot.*

No, he's not. He's mean.

"Here." Muscles pulled my dagger from his belt and sliced through the rope. It tumbled to the ground, and I rubbed the raw skin at my wrists. "Was that painful?"

"I've been tied up all day," I pointed out. "Got any lotion?"

Erik tilted his head, so his hair cascaded over his shoulder. "Lotion?"

"Never mind," I said hastily. "I'll be fine."

Erik took my wrists in his hands and rubbed lightly. The now-familiar heat built slowly from the inside, ebbing lower until it pulsed just below my navel.

Stop it, Saga. Don't be that girl. Kick him and run.

No. Don't run. Dragons.

It would always come back to the dragons. *Skit.*

Erik lowered his head. "I am sorry you were uncomfortable."

"Thanks."

Erik's gaze met mine. His eyes were so intense, I could have been consumed by their endless blue depths. My vision swam, lightheadedness overtaking me until I swayed.

"You're not well," Erik deduced.

"It's just been a really long day, okay?"

Not wanting to embarrass myself further, I turned on one heel and walked onto the porch. Erik hadn't been wrong about the weather—a light wind now lapped the air, and the sky had clouded over. A storm was definitely coming. Resolved, I loaded my arms with logs, and turned back to the door. I entered to find Erik frowning.

"You need to eat," he deduced. "Give those to me."

"I'm fine." I placed the logs into his outstretched arms.

"You haven't had anything all day—not since I met you, at any rate. You have to be hungry." Erik deposited the wood by the fireplace, then crossed to the corner that served as a kitchen. He opened a cupboard and pulled down a loaf of bread and some dried fruit. At my raised brow, he explained, "We stocked the cabin on our way in. Since we didn't have much business to conduct, we figured it might be a short trip."

"Planning paid off." It usually did.

"Eat," Erik ordered.

At the sight of the food, my stomach rumbled. I gave in, sitting at one of the benches lining the farm table before looking up at Erik. "Oh. Am I supposed to serve it to you?"

Erik carried the food to the table and sat opposite me. He broke off a hunk of bread and handed it across the table. "Clan Bjorn's as bad as they say, eh?"

My teeth sank into the crust with more ferocity than I intended. "You have no idea," I mumbled through a mouthful of crumbs.

"Mmm." Erik stroked his beard. He didn't speak again, just nudged the fruit across the table and broke off a piece of bread for himself. We ate in silence, until nothing but crumbs remained on the table.

"We have more," Erik offered.

But I shook my head. "I'm fine. Thanks for dinner."

Erik's gaze moved to my wrists, still raw from the ropes. I rubbed them self-consciously, then brought my hands to my mouth as a yawn overtook me.

"Go to bed," Erik ordered. "I'll keep the fire going."

"I thought you wanted help."

He shook his head. "You need rest. Tomorrow will be a full day."

Oh, God. "A lot more travel?"

"*Ja.* And an evening of introductions. You'll find your new home to be . . . vast." Erik stood and stalked toward the fire. I tried not to stare at the way his butt flexed against his leather pants.

God. Seriously, Saga?

"What's it like?" I hedged. "Valkyris?"

Erik added another log to the flames, then leaned against the far end of the dining table. "You'll see."

I rubbed at my wrists. "And how long am I to stay there?"

Erik's brows shot to his hairline. "Do you want to return to Clan Bjorn?"

"No! I'm just . . ." I shrugged, helplessly. "This is all new to me."

"Sleep." Erik ran a hand through his hair again. "You'll have answers tomorrow."

With a nod, I stood and crossed to the bed.

To the one bed.

I hovered anxiously beside it. "Um . . ."

"There's a nightdress in the trunk." Erik angled his chin toward a wooden box. "I'll look away if you wish to change."

"And, uh . . . you're sleeping . . . where?"

"There's a reindeer pelt in the trunk as well. Leave it out, and I'll make a spot by the fire."

"You're going to sleep on the floor?" I stared at the wooden slats.

"Unless you'd rather I share your bed."

"No!" I squeaked. "Okay, turn around!"

Something akin to amusement sparked in Erik's eyes as he lowered himself onto the bench and sat facing the fire. I removed my shoes and undid the endless number of ties on the back of my dress, then shimmied into the thickest, puffiest nightgown I'd ever seen. With its bulbous sleeves, frilly hem, and an absurd amount of ribbons, it looked like something Mormor's mormor might have worn.

To a medieval costume party.

Snort.

I pulled the requested reindeer pelt out of the trunk, and set it on the edge of the table. Then, I climbed into bed and slipped under the thick, furry pelt that served as my blanket, vowing never again to take for granted the miracle of modern bedding. *If I'm lucky enough to see it again.* With the animal hide pulled all the way up to my chin, I called out, "It's clear!"

Erik turned, angling his shoulders to me. "Sleep well, uh . . . you haven't told me your name."

"Saga," I offered. "My name is Saga Skånstad."

One corner of Erik's mouth turned up in a smile. "Sleep well, Saga Skånstad."

He stood to stoke the fire, giving me another shot of his absolutely spectacular butt.

My dreams that night were *extremely* pleasant.

CHAPTER 7

I AWOKE TO THE absolutely delightful smell of fish, and bread, and . . . oh my God, was it . . . I sat straight up in bed. "Are you making coffee?"

Erik glanced over his shoulder. "I'm preparing tea. And fish and toasted bread. I hope it's enough—I saw what you did to the food last night."

"Hey," I protested. But it was impossible to be annoyed when a six-and-a-half foot, shirtless Viking was making me breakfast.

Hold the phone. A shirtless Viking . . . *yum.* Erik's bare chest was even more beautiful than his leather-clad butt. And I should know—my dreams had been filled with nothing else.

"Where'd you get all this food?" I climbed out of bed and walked toward the kitchen.

"The fish I caught from the stream this morning. Everything else, my father and I brought on our ride in."

"And you know how to cook it?" So much for my theory that Viking men were useless in all things but pillaging.

Erik shot me a strange look. "We're going to eat it, aren't we?"

"I just meant that, well . . . in that other tribe I was with, the women did all of the cooking. Actually, they did everything but the heavy farm work and the, uh, killing."

Erik's eyes darkened. He turned to stare intently at the fish atop the flame. "Bjorn engages in unfortunate practices. We have left them on their own for many years, but a visit might be in order."

"Do you have any power over them?" I asked. "I thought the tribes were autonomous."

"They are. For the most part." Erik removed the pans from the flame. He transferred the food to plates and set them on the table before retrieving two cups of tea. "But it is the gods-given responsibility of the most powerful tribe to enforce the higher laws. When a clan oversteps the bounds of basic human decency, well . . ." Erik sat on one of the benches and motioned for me to do the same.

"Send in the dragons?" I joked. I reached across the table, gratefully accepting the offered tea.

And then I took a drink.

"My God," I squawked as the foul-tasting liquid slid down my throat. "What is this?"

"It's tea."

"It's bitter!"

"Because it's tea." From Erik's expression, I may as well have grown two heads.

Right. When in Vikingdom, drink as the Vikings do.

Except that this tea was *really gross*.

"Do you have any, uh . . . sweetener?" I asked.

"There may be honey in the cupboard, but—"

"Great!" I jumped up. A small amount of digging revealed a tiny container, the contents of which I eagerly spooned into my tea. When I drank again, the tea went down more smoothly. "Sorry. You were talking about enforcing laws?"

Erik's eyes danced with amusement. "I was. But now I'm curious, what do you drink, if not tea?"

"Coffee," I said. *Duh.*

"I'm not familiar with that."

"Seriously? You guys don't have *any* coffee here? That stinks!"

"Pardon?"

"Not you. You don't stink. You smell great. Like pine. I mean, uh . . ." Heat flooded my cheeks as I clamped my lips shut. I took a deep breath before opening my mouth again. "I just mean coffee is fantastic, and if you ever have the chance to try some, you're going to be *really* happy."

Especially after a lifetime of drinking this horrid tea.

"I'll take your word for it. Now please eat, Saga. We have a long day ahead."

Right.

I tucked into my food, savoring the fresh fish and

pan-seared bread with a newfound appreciation. My time in the slave quarters had given me a solid respect for all non-gruel-based food products.

When we'd finished breakfast, I washed the dishes in the stream while Erik prepared his horse for our journey. Dreams of escape danced through my head, but the threat of airborne sentries was enough to keep me tethered to the property.

When our work was finished, we dressed, climbed onto the horse, and rode through the mountains toward the mysterious fortress of Valkyris. The ground was muddy from the previous night's rain but the horse trod easily through the slippery terrain, making what I guessed was good time. Erik didn't complain, at any rate.

We paused at the base of yet another fjord, and I scanned the shoreline. "Is this it?"

"No." Erik slid off the horse and led us to a raft. "One more transport."

"That floating pile of sticks?" I crossed my arms. If he thought that paltry thing would support the two of us plus a horse, he'd clearly fallen out of the stupid tree and hit every branch.

Good thing I was a strong swimmer.

"Trust me?" Erik glanced over his shoulder, his sky-blue eyes piercing mine.

"Whatever."

Erik led us to the raft. I gripped the horse's mane, anticipating its resistance to stepping onto what was clearly a death trap. But the horse followed Erik onto the logs with ease. Erik untied the moorings, and we drifted smoothly from the shore.

"Did you forget something?" I mimed rowing. We were literally up a creek—well, a fjord—without a paddle.

Erik eyed me steadily. "I think we'll make it."

"How? How are we possibly going to get anywhere without an oar?" Maybe he really did have a run-in with the stupid tree.

The cute ones were always the dumbest.

"You said you'd trust me," Erik reminded me.

"Yeah, well that was before I realized you were the one Viking who knows absolutely nothing about water travel!"

Erik turned so his back was to me. He looked to the top of the nearest mountain—a steep, tree-lined slope with a light dusting of snow at its tip. When a light flashed from the top of the peak, Erik cupped his hands to his mouth and shouted, "Torbin! Send them down!"

"Send who down? Who's Torbin?"

"We really need to work on those trust issues, Saga."

"I—oh my God!" I shrieked as two massive, winged reptiles crested over the top of the mountain. The dragons swooped gracefully across the sky before angling their heads downward and diving.

Straight for the raft.

"Arugh!" I pressed myself flat against the horse's back and covered my head. "Erik, do something!"

"What would you have me do?" Erik sounded far more relaxed than the circumstances warranted.

"I don't know! Slay them!"

"Slay them?" Erik's voice positively brimmed with humor.

"Do something!" I shrieked again.

"If you insist." I opened one eye just enough to see Erik place his fingers between his lips. A low whistle pierced the air, and seconds later, a wind whipped fiercely at my back. The raft surged forward, seemingly carried on the breeze.

Which was all well and good, except that there were still two enormous, carnivorous *dragons* coming straight for us. Or . . . I glanced up at the now-empty sky, then craned my neck to look over my shoulder.

A scream of terror ripped from my throat. "They're right behind us!"

"I'm aware."

"Why aren't you terrified?"

"Saga," Erik said patiently, "as you pointed out, we have no oar. How did you think we were going to get across this fjord?"

"Not by dragon!" I blinked at the sight of the two beasts flapping their wings and stirring the water with their tails. They guided us forward with ease, and despite my extremely logical fear, they didn't seem inclined to eat us. *How is this actually happening?*

"Dragons need purpose," Erik offered. "These two have served as Valkyris escorts since before I was born."

"And they haven't eaten anyone?" I hadn't released my hold on the poor horse.

"No one that we didn't want them to," Erik said.

His face was so impassive, I couldn't tell whether he was kidding.

I looked over my shoulder again, shuddering at the thick, black talons hovering just above the water. The dragon's synchronized flaps seemed controlled enough, but if one pushed forward just a bit I'd be a human-kebab in the time it took me to say *Erik, for the love of God, just slay the—*

A fierce shudder wracked my spine, and I buried my head against the horse's neck. "Tell me when it's over," I begged.

Erik placed one hand over mine and squeezed gently. We rode in silence for the rest of the trip, the only sounds the lapping of the waves and the flapping of the wings. After what felt like an eternity, the raft jerked unsteadily.

"You can open your eyes. We're here."

With my cheek still pressed against the horse's neck, I opened one eye to find the dragons hovering at the side of the boat. Erik pointed two fingers and circled his arm to the left, and the dragons soared mercifully away.

"They listen to you?" I balked.

"I should hope so." Erik slipped the hand not holding mine against the small of my back. He guided me off the horse, earning points for not laughing when my knees buckled.

It had been one hell of a ride.

"Now what?" I righted myself and folded my hands at my waist.

"Now we go home." Erik led the horse off the raft and onto the rocky shore. I followed a few steps behind, stepping through the seagrass and pausing to finger a cluster of heather. The beach felt strangely familiar . . . The shoreline curving along the island, and the mixture of wildflowers and deciduous trees dotting the nearby knoll, seemed like things I'd seen before. In all my Norwegian summers, I'd never visited anywhere this remote, but still . . .

Maybe I'd dreamed about it.

"Saga?" Erik looked down from the top of the hill. "Are you coming?"

"Yes. Right." I lifted my skirt and hurried after Erik. When I reached the top of the hill, my eyes widened, my lips parted, and I emitted a sound Mormor would have deemed undignified.

But holy *skit*. This place . . .

Erik placed his hand on the small of my back again and said simply, "*Velkommen* to Valkyris."

CHAPTER 8

"**T**HIS IS YOUR HOME?**" The words came out on a squawk. After two weeks shackled inside a windowless hut, and a night spent in a cabin in the woods, I certainly hadn't expected, well . . . *this.*

"It's comfortable." Erik shrugged.

"It's a *castle,*" I corrected. And it was—a multi-storied, four-towered, turret-boasting, *castle*. One that could have been ripped from the pages of a fairytale with fields of blooms bordering its walls, and large windows framing either side of the heavily guarded front door. Wide, cream-colored stones made up the bulk of the structure, with iron candle-fixtures attached at twenty foot intervals along the ground floor. Higher up, walkways connected the four towers, the blue tiles of their roofs a near perfect match for Erik's eyes.

Not that I noticed.

"What's over there?" I pointed to the left of the

67

castle, where a second, slightly smaller stone structure stood.

"The Dragehus," Erik said.

Crazy-hot Viking said what? "Pardon?"

"The stable where we keep the dragons," he explained.

Right.

Behind the Dragehus was an enormous field. It stretched from the knolls behind the dragon barn across the island, where its grassy turf gave way to a series of plots. There, crops sprung from the earth, farmers tilled the ground, and a group of children skipped after an exuberant dog.

"Do you have many other animals here? Besides the, uh, dragons?"

"We keep our domestic animals on the opposite side of the main structure." Erik pointed to the right of the castle, where a third stone building was bordered by a vast pasture. Cows, sheep, goats, and chickens roamed freely atop a lush bed of greenery.

What kept the dragons from eating them?

Between the structures was another massive field. This one was set up with archery targets, nets, and what appeared to be some kind of a fighting ring.

"And behind the pasture is the craftsman's structure." Erik pointed again. "Come. I'll show you around."

Erik pulled his horse forward, and I followed him along the winding path to the castle. As we approached, a young boy jumped over the pasture's fence and ran toward us.

"Welcome home, sir." The boy bowed. "I'll take your horse for you."

"Thank you, Langley. He's been traveling for several days, so check his hooves then let him rest." Erik handed the rope to the boy, who bowed again before leading the horse toward the barn. Erik continued toward the castle and I followed, trying not to gawk at the tapestry of yellow and purple wildflowers lining the walkway. Either the land was just that good, or Valkyris employed some seriously gifted gardeners.

"Sir." The six guards framing the castle's massive front door brought their fists to their chests in unison. "*Velkommen.*"

Erik nodded, and two of the guards stepped forward to open the door. The wood was so thick, it groaned with the movement. Erik crossed over the threshold, and I picked at my cuticles as I followed him into the vast entry. Intricately woven tapestries in shades of blue and cream lined the walls, and buttercup-filled vases sat atop elegant wooden tables. Corridors stretched to the left and the right, each boasting windows that filled the space with light. A grand staircase ran from the polished floor to the second story, where a white-pillared railing bordered a long hallway. The entire room was illuminated by candles that burned in ornate chandeliers and wall sconces. The flames were reflected in large mirrors placed opposite the windows, making the already substantial space seem absolutely enormous.

"I cannot believe you live here," I whispered.

Erik crossed to one of the vases and pulled out a flower. Rough fingers stroked the delicate stem as he looked over at me and shrugged. "It's just a home, Saga."

Watching him stand in the entry, sword and dagger at his hip and a flower in his hand, I had the most peculiar sensation of *déjà vu.* The room, the moment . . . all of it was disconcertingly familiar. The feeling washed over me as my eyes locked on Erik's, and I knew with absolute certainty that I was going to be okay here. Maybe not comfortable. Maybe not even happy. But okay.

It would have to be enough.

"My son! You're home!" A warm voice rang from the upper level. I tore my eyes from Erik's to find a breathtakingly beautiful woman descending the staircase. Her white-blond hair was swept into an intricate braid that highlighted elegant cheekbones and sparkling blue eyes. She wore an ivory gown with silver-blue snowflakes stitched from one shoulder all the way down to the hem. Her movements were so fluid she appeared to float, rather than walk, down the stairs.

When she reached the bottom, Erik dipped his head and offered her the flower. "I selected it for you, Mother."

"From the bouquet I picked this morning?" Erik's mom raised one arched brow.

"Precisely," Erik said. "I knew it would be to your liking."

His mother tilted her head back, her laughter filling the room. "I am very glad to see you home. I always worry about the *Ting*. Blood feuds and ale are a poor combination."

"Agreed. But I'm here. And I have what you requested." Erik withdrew my dagger from his belt, and offered it to his mother. "I return it to your care, safe and sound."

Wait. What? My dagger belonged to Erik's *mom*?

"Thank you. I'll lock this away for safekeeping." She slipped the dagger into the pocket of her dress, and turned to face me. "And you, my dear. We are most pleased that you have come to join us."

Huh? Why was she being so nice to me?

"Thank you, uh . . ." I wasn't sure how to address Erik's mom. She was the wife of a chief, but she lived in what seemed to be a castle. Was she a chieftess, or a queen, or . . . I pressed my lips together. There were no etiquette books that covered this.

"Oh, forgive me. I forget, this is all new to you." Erik's mom reached out to clasp my hands in hers. "I am Chieftess Freia—founder of the Valkyris Tribe, and guardian of this island."

Hold on. Erik's tribe was led by a woman? His mom had created this whole fantastical world?

"I—erm, I . . ." I dropped into an awkward curtsy. "It's a pleasure to meet you, Your Highness, uh, Your Excellency, er . . . ma'am?"

"No need for that." Freia placed a hand to my elbow and guided me up. "It is *my* pleasure to welcome you to

Valkyris. I'm not sure what my son has told you about us, but I hope you will come to love this land as your own." Freia leaned closer, her eyes filled with warmth.

My gaze flickered to Erik, who shot Freia a stern look. "Mother."

Freia waved him away. "The girl needs to know what she's gotten herself into."

"'The girl' has been taken captive twice. What she needs is the chance to acclimate to all of this." Erik waved a hand in the air. I tried not to notice the way his biceps flexed with the movement.

I failed.

"Erik." Freia smiled. "Why don't you check in on our newborns? Two of the dragon eggs hatched while you were away, and I know you prefer to bond with them as early as possible."

"Trying to get rid of me so you can convert Saga?" Erik raised a brow.

Hold up. Is this a cult?

"Saga." Freia smiled. "Such a beautiful name."

"Thank you," I whispered.

"Mother?" Erik pressed.

"I promise to go easy on our guest." Freia raised her right hand. "Now go play with your dragons. Your father sent word that he will arrive soon, and we can catch up then."

"Very well. Mother." Erik bowed his head. "Saga."

"Erik." I nodded back.

He gave me one more look before turning and

stalking down one of the corridors. I *definitely* did not stare at his butt as he walked away.

Well, not for long.

"You are fond of my son." Freia's voice interrupted my ogling.

"What? Oh." Mortification doused my lust. "No. It's not like that. He's just . . . Well, he's the first person who's been . . . not awful to me in this whole . . ." Whole timeline? Whole alternate universe? What could I possibly say that wouldn't make me seem totally crazy? "In this whole place," I finished lamely.

"You must have been through quite the ordeal." Freia clucked her tongue. "Did Erik say you were taken captive twice?"

"Yeah." I sighed. "Erik captured me when I was trying to run from Bjorn—I was supposed to marry their heir."

"Oh." Freia's brows furrowed. "I didn't mean for that to happen. I'm so sorry, Saga. I fear that was quite my fault."

My breath hitched. "What do you mean?"

"It's a rather involved story." Freia linked her arm through mine. "Come, dear. We'll take a walk. You need to understand your place in all of this."

"All of this?"

"Our tribe. Our world. Saga, it was not circumstance that brought you here. It was Fate." My chest tightened as Freia tilted her head and said, "Our people have been waiting for you for a very long time."

CHAPTER 9

"WHAT DOES THAT MEAN?" I asked.

"I suppose I should start at the beginning. We'll walk while we talk." Freia led us down the corridor Erik had taken—the one that led to a dragon nursery. *Gulp.*

"The Valkyris Tribe was founded on the principles of enlightenment and equality—values once important to our society, but forgotten as procurement of lands and wealth became the driving force. I was born into a tribe that valued riches above all else—it certainly didn't value women, or believe we had the capacity to contribute in any way. I spent my formative years alternately oppressed and abused, and though those practices broke my sisters and many of my friends, I dreamed of a different life." Freia paused at an open doorway, giving me a chance to glance in at the sitting area. Instruments lined one wall, while padded chairs and floor pillows rested against the other.

"That sounds terrible," I murmured. "I'm sorry you experienced that."

"It's no worse than what you must have seen during your time with Clan Bjorn," Freia said. "And I did what you must have done—I fought for the life I knew I deserved. I refused to let them destroy my spirit. At every crossroads I chose hope, driven by the unwavering knowledge that someday, my life would be my own. When the opportunity finally presented itself, I ran away."

"Were you afraid they would catch you?"

"Of course." Freia continued walking until she reached another door. Inside were chairs, cushions, and shelves bearing bound parchments—a library! "But I was more fearful of what would happen to me if I stayed."

"So, you ran to this island?" I asked.

"Not exactly. I ran to the woods . . . and straight into a feral wolf. It attacked, leaping from behind a tree before I ever knew it was there. I had no weapon, no means of escape. I was as good as dead . . . or I would have been, had Halvar not saved me."

"What happened?" I followed Freia from the library past another staircase, glancing curiously up it. This one appeared more utilitarian than the one in the entry.

"That leads to the staff quarters," Freia offered. "The second story is largely work spaces and meeting rooms, while the third houses living quarters. Our governing families live in residential suites just off the main entrance."

"Got it." I fingered the hem of my sleeve as we walked onward.

"Halvar killed the wolf—he's an excellent archer. I was badly shaken when he approached, and terrified of what he intended to do with me. I hadn't been brought up to expect kindness from men, but Halvar showed me only compassion. When he learned where I'd come from, he never once thought to return me, though he knew that harboring a female from my tribe would be automatic grounds for a blood feud. Instead, he asked what I wanted my life to be . . . and from that day forward, he set about helping me to build just that."

At the end of the hallway we turned, pausing to let a group of women pass. They had fabric in their arms and smiles on their faces, and when they rounded the corner, they scurried up the staircase we'd just passed.

"Our seamstresses," Freia explained. "Valkyris garments are revered through Norway for their quality and artistry. I know you've come without a wardrobe of your own—if you tell me the styles you favor, I'll have some dresses made for you."

"Thank you. That's really kind."

Freia reached over to squeeze my hand. "Kindness is the single greatest gift we can offer. My parents named me for Freya, the Goddess of Love, and so long as I act from that virtue, it is *always* returned to me . . . and multiplied into the world. Had Halvar not shown me kindness that day in the woods, none of this would exist."

"So how did the—"

"General Freia!" I was interrupted by the cry of a woman. She strode toward us, sword in one hand and shield in the other. Long red hair streamed behind her as she called out, "There has been a breach."

General?

"Where?" My host withdrew her hand and turned her attention to the seeming-soldier in front of her. But women couldn't be warriors—could they?

"The south mountain." The woman sheathed her sword. "Torbin spotted two men at the edge of the fjord. He redirected the raft so they couldn't arrange transport, but their proximity is unprecedented."

"Nobody has ever reached the edge of the water-way." Freia turned to me. "Valkyris is meant to be unlocatable."

Oh.

"They must have followed Erik," Freia said.

"Or Chief Halvar," the woman suggested. "He is due to return soon. It's possible the intruders followed him from the *Ting*."

"If they've discovered the passage, they cannot be allowed to return home." Freia pressed her fingertips together. "Send one of the riders to engage them. The goal should be conversion, but if they're unwilling, I'm afraid they'll need to be killed."

"As you wish, General." The woman bowed her head before hastening down the hallway.

Freia returned her attention to me. "I don't often order executions, but in this case, it will likely be necessary."

I chewed on my bottom lip. "I really don't understand what's going on. Are you the Chieftess or the General or . . ."

"Both." Freia hooked her arm through mine again and led us down the corridor. When we reached a display of helmets, we turned and entered a large ballroom. A chandelier was suspended from the ceiling, its outsides laden with crystals and what looked suspiciously like flameless candles. But that wasn't possible—those wouldn't be invented for hundreds of years.

Right?

"After Halvar saved me from the wolf, he brought me back to his village. He came from a fishing community that inhabited a string of islands just off the coast. His tribesmen were nothing like the men I'd grown up with. They were gentle, and honest. They took pride in their work, and revered *all* forms of life—women and children included. They were good-hearted and fair, and when Halvar told them of the society I wished to build—one in which women played key roles, and every member was respected for their contribution—they agreed to help. We established Valkyris the following year—we discovered this island and made it our new home. We knew it was important that we maintained the outward appearance of ferocity—as we grew in strength and influence, clans would seek to take our land. And so, we acquired warriors—brutal fighters from faraway tribes who wanted better lives. Most of our founding members were too peaceful to lead an army, so I became Valkyris' general. Now I perform both roles—general of our army, and co-chief of our tribe, alongside my husband."

I eyed Freia with admiration. "You created the life you wanted to live."

"Isn't that what we're all called to do?" Freia studied the chandelier. "Bring about the change we wish to see in our world?"

"Well, yeah, but . . ." I toed the ballroom floor. "Most of us don't pull it off."

"Perhaps." Freia resumed walking. "But the power to do so lies within each of us."

God, I wished. Here Freia had conjured an entire society, and I couldn't even figure out how to get myself home.

Life goals.

When we reached the far side of the ballroom, Freia led us through a double door and down another corridor. Eight-foot paintings lined the wall to our left, while massive windows looked onto the open courtyard to our right. The outdoor walkway gave way to two steps leading to a sunken lawn, where well-manicured grass was broken up by a series of gardens. A rose maze took up one quadrant, while the opposite corner boasted stone benches hidden behind tall bursts of lavender. Freia walked us down the hallway and turned into another room. With its long tables and polished benches, it had to be the dining hall.

"So," I hedged. "Valkyris pretends to be merciless raiders to the outside world, but in reality, you're an egalitarian society?"

"Exactly. I have no patience for the brutalities I witnessed as a child, nor do I permit them within my borders. We do what we must to protect our way of life, but beyond that I do not stand for violence or intolerance of any kind. You'll find many lifestyles are celebrated here, and religious freedoms respected. We worship both the pantheon of old, and the Christian ideals now spreading through the land. So long as our residents revere kindness, honor, and decency, they are encouraged to conduct their personal lives as they see fit."

Sounded like the equality my present-day country was *still* shooting for. *Well done, Viking lady.*

We reached the back of the dining hall. Freia pointed to her left, where a massive kitchen housed countless pots, pans, hearths, and a row of open flames that looked like the precursor to the modern stove. Cooks stood over the fires, preparing what I could only guess was the evening meal. My stomach rumbled at the smell of roasting meat, and I hastily pressed my hands to my midsection.

"Oh, dear," Freia rued. "I should have offered you something to eat."

"I'm fine," I lied.

My stomach outed me. Again.

"Celine," Freia called to a matronly woman chopping vegetables. "Please prepare two meals and send them up to our new guest's quarters in the students' wing."

"Right away, ma'am." Celine retrieved two plates from a cupboard, and placed generous hunks of bread and cheese on each of them. "The hot food will be ready in half an hour—would you like these sent up first?"

"No. But we will take some bread with us." Freia entered the kitchen and pointed to a stack of small, round rolls. "Are these already accounted for?"

"Help yourself," Celine said. "We've just baked a fresh batch."

"Wonderful." Freia picked up two rolls and cupped them in her hands. "Thank you, Celine."

"It's my pleasure, ma'am." Celine returned to her chopping while Freia joined me in the dining hall. She handed me one of the rolls, and raised the other in a toast. "Not to boast, but our bakers make some of the finest bread in all of Norway."

My stomach emitted a roar of approval, sending a shot of embarrassment straight to my heated face. "Sorry," I murmured.

Freia leaned closer with a conspiratorial smile. "Our bakers would consider that high praise. Come, we'll eat while we walk."

I waited until Freia took a bite, before giving my stomach what it so desperately wanted. My fish breakfast may as well have been a lifetime ago. I inhaled, rather than savored, my roll, then hurriedly followed Freia down yet another corridor.

"This place is huge," I said.

"We've nearly completed the tour. The upper floors, as I've said, are largely workspaces and private residences. This is the wing where you'll be spending much of your time." Freia stepped into one last corridor. This one had the same courtyard view to one side. Opposite was a wall of mirrors, all leading to a set of thick, wooden doors. The carvings on the doors bore the same details as those on the front of the castle—entwined cords wove through leaping dragons, meeting in the center to encircle a magnificent tree. Inside the circle was an iron plate with gold runic inscriptions.

"This is beautiful." I brushed my fingers over the ancient letters. "What does it say?"

"You can't read?" Freia inquired.

"I can read, um"—*English!*—"modern letters."

"But not the runes. Hmm. We'll remedy that."

Oh, God. I'd been here all of twenty minutes and I'd already disappointed my host. "I'm a fast learner," I offered.

"I'm sure you are." Freia's eyes crinkled in a smile. "The runes say, 'Within these doors lie seekers of wisdom.' This portion of the castle is our educational facility. Here, we train our youth in the ways of the *virtuous* explorer."

My fingertips stilled. "It's a school."

"Yes." Freia folded her hands at her waist. "And a very fine one, at that."

"Are women allowed to attend?" It seemed logical given all she'd told me, but I didn't want to presume.

Freia arched one perfectly groomed brow. "On Valkyris, women are accorded equal rights and opportunities to our male counterparts. It is my firm belief that a good education is the single most important tool an individual can possess."

On that point, Freia and my grandmother were definitely of one mind. My heart tugged at the thought of Mormor. She'd have given anything to see this place; to soak in its history. And right then, I'd have given anything to see *her*.

God, I miss my family so much.

"Saga?" Freia's voice pulled me from my pity party.

"Mmm? Sorry. I agree. About education, I mean. It's very important." I folded my hands, mirroring Freia's posture. "This is just . . . different from the last place I lived."

"Clan Bjorn has worrisome views about the role of females." Freia frowned. "But that is for my council to resolve. You, my dear, have other matters to attend to. When Halvar and I established this society, we knew our survival depended on training the next generation of leaders. We started out small, but as time went on and we acquired more residents, we realized that a formalized education would serve not only our youth, but the tribe as a whole. We selected our faculty from among the most skilled craftsmen, warriors, and artisans Valkyris had to offer. Those individuals teach the skills our people were *meant* to share—ship building, seafaring, navigation, weaving, carving, ironwork, and storytelling. We were never meant to be the vicious pirates we have become. We were meant to share our knowledge with the world—and to return home with a greater awareness of art, food, architecture, and culture. We were *always* meant to disseminate that information throughout our land, bringing Norway into a brighter, more enlightened future."

Freia spoke so earnestly, I didn't have the heart to tell her the truth—that although Vikings would be revered through history for their unparalleled ship-building and death-defying voyages, they would be most remembered for their piracy, thievery and brutality.

The very things she was fighting against.

"So, this school." I fingered the fabric of my dress. "What happens after the students are trained?"

"They take apprenticeships in their chosen field, and put their skills to use for the betterment of the tribe. We have many disciplines—from animal care and dragon training, to shipbuilding and navigation, to archery and combat. Valkyris is not without its army, and we pride ourselves on having never lost a battle." Freia smiled. "Though the dragons do help tip our hand."

"So the whole 'Valkyris is a brutish tribe of savages' reputation . . . it really is just an act."

"Correct. We've found that clans respond more favorably to a language they already speak. In this day and age, that language seems to be unbridled violence."

"General Freia!" Footsteps pounded on the polished floor as the same redheaded warrior ran down the hallway. "The intruders have refused conversion . . . and they're putting up a terrible fight. They took shelter in an outcropping below our lookout. When they spotted the rider, they fired on Torbin. The rider tried to intercept the arrows, but his dragon wasn't fast enough, and Torbin . . . perished."

Freia's hand fluttered to her heart. "Gone so young."

"My sorrow for your loss." The warrior bowed her head. "What would you have us do?"

"Killing a sentinel is automatic grounds for a blood feud—something of which the intruders were no doubt advised. One of the tribes must be seeking war," Freia surmised.

"Or trying to pull you out of hiding," I hedged. "This land is kept secret, right?"

Freia turned to me. "What are you thinking, Saga?"

"Well, Erik just stole me from the most aggressive heir in the history of ever. Then he took off before Lars could retaliate. Maybe *Lars* sent those two scouts to figure out where Erik lives . . . and exact revenge."

Freia's lips pressed together in a tight line. "You have the mind of a strategist, Saga." She turned her attention back to the warrior. "Obviously, the intruders must now be killed," Freia said calmly. "But send an interrogator to extract as much information from them as possible, first. Fetch Erik from the Dragehus—if the intruders are reluctant to speak, he'll find a way to break them."

85

I bit down on the inside of my cheek. The guy who'd cooked me breakfast was a breaker of people. I really knew how to pick 'em.

"I'll send Erik immediately." The warrior gave a tight nod. "Shall I dispatch another rider to accompany him?"

"Yes. Preferably one skilled at long-range execution. If the interrogation goes wrong, I want my son protected from the sky as well as the ground. Are any of our archers available?"

"Those numbers dipped after our last conflict," the warrior said. "We have only two master archers remaining."

"Send the best available," Freia ordered. "And hurry."

"Yes, General." The warrior ran down the hallway, leaving me with one concerned General and a million unanswered questions.

"I hadn't realized our numbers had fallen so low." Freia spoke softly.

"I'm pretty handy with a bow and arrow," I offered. "Maybe I can help."

"Think you can learn to shoot while riding a dragon?"

"Well, uh . . ."

Freia frowned. "Come, Saga. If you are going to be of use to us, we must commence your indoctrination."

I wrung my hands together. "What do you expect of me?"

"I expect you to apply yourself to your studies—to

utilize that strategist's mind by learning the ways of our tribe."

"You want me to . . . to study?" A magic dagger ripped me through a thousand-year wormhole so I could *keep going to school*? The universe had a majorly twisted sense of humor.

"How else will you learn the ways of Valkyris?" Freia arched her brow. "And without learning our ways, how will you lead us?"

Lead you? What about going home? How long am I going to be stuck here?

I leaned against the thick door for support. "You want *me* to lead? You don't know anything about me. Why would you trust me with your tribe?"

"I'm trusting my *son* with my tribe," Freia corrected. "Erik was not born to be our leader, but like all of us, he must adapt to life's changes."

Huh?

"When Halvar and I established this society, we agreed that balance was the key to successful governance. One day my son will become Chief—a *male* chief, who may or may not elect to marry. And when he does, he will need a team of strong *female* leaders to guide him. I expect you to become one of those leaders, Saga."

No! No leading anyone! I want to go home!

I drew a shaky breath. "Why me? Of all the girls here, and all the girls in your allied tribes, and all the girls in the whole entire world, why would you want *me*? I'm a stranger." *A stranger from another time!*

"Because the dagger chose you," Freia said calmly. "I asked the blade to bring us an ideal Valkyris leader, and it brought you. The gods are never wrong, Saga. You were fated to lead us—whether as an officer of our army, or one of our explorers, or one of our prophets, I don't yet know. I only know that the dagger selected *you.*"

Holy. Freaking. *Skit.*

My throat clenched at her words—words that implied I might never see my family again. If I was fated to lead here, what the hell did that mean for my other life? My *real* life?

Am I going to be stuck here forever?

A few weeks ago, I'd been about to start my freshman year of college in a world with cars and computers and space travel. Now, I was an unwitting future leader of a secret tribe, embarking on a course of study that ranged from weaving to shipbuilding to war-strategizing. *A thousand years in my past.*

Whether I liked it or not, I was about to enroll in what I could only describe as Viking Academy. My life was completely out of control.

CHAPTER 10

"COME, SAGA. I'LL SHOW you Valkyris Academy," Freia said.

Valkyris. Not Viking. *Right.*

Freia pulled the double doors open and stepped into a space that positively bubbled with excitement. Chatter bounced off the high ceilings of what appeared to be a social area, where students had claimed spots around circular tables and atop plush floor pillows. Boys and girls streamed through the open doors at the back of the space, spilling onto the grass where groups socialized over afternoon tea. The whole place was charged with a joy I hadn't experienced since I'd touched the dagger. Viking Academy was . . .

It was happy.

I wished Ingrid and Vidia could have been here with me. And Olivia and Mormor . . .

God, I miss them.

"It's . . . lovely," I whispered.

"It is," Freia said proudly. "Halvar and I spent a great deal of time arranging this space. We knew socialization would be every bit as important to our students' learning as academic preparation, so we designed the wing to foster interaction."

She crossed the room, and I hurried after her.

"Since I must return to tribal business, I'll make the rest of our tour brief. On the third floor you'll find student living quarters—including your room, and the student dining hall. Of course, you're welcome to come to the formal dining room in the main part of the castle, but most students find it easier to eat in this wing between classes. As for the first floor, classrooms are to the left. Weaving, sewing, and domestic arts are practiced in these rooms." Freia nodded at a series of open doors, through which cheery chatter emerged. "Over here, you'll study with scribes, storytellers, and dramatists—those who pass our history along through the written and spoken word."

"Very nice." I peered into the classrooms, taking in the rows of tables where students scribbled away with feather pens, and the raised stage where two girls were engaged in some kind of a performance.

"Down here, you'll find our agricultural classrooms and our woodcarving and blacksmith workshops. The more involved projects are completed in the outbuildings. The second story is home to our divinity department—prophesying and religion are taught there—as well as some of our history and diplomacy courses. And at the opposite end of this wing, on both the first and second floors, we have our physical combat classes. Swordsmanship and other more aggressive methods of defense are taught on the first floor, while strategy is learned on the second."

"Wow," I whispered. "This is amazing."

Freia smiled. "Let's take you up to your room. I've arranged a private suite, since I'm sure this is a bit . . . overwhelming."

She didn't know the half of it.

"Um . . ." I hedged as I followed Freia up the stairs. "Can I ask you about something you said earlier?"

"Of course."

"You said that you'd sent that dagger to bring you the 'ideal Valkyris leader.' I don't understand . . . how could a dagger bring me to you?"

"Ah." Freia paused, seeming to search for words. "I'm sure you've noticed that some of the features of this castle seem rather . . . advanced, for our time. The glass in the windows, the flameless candles? And you haven't seen the bucket-less bathing chambers."

Oh, thank God. If this place had indoor plumbing, even the poor-man's medieval version, I would be inordinately grateful.

"I did." I nodded.

"You'll learn that our society has been blessed by the gods," Freia resumed climbing the staircase.

What?

"When Halvar and I chose this island, we walked every inch on foot, determined to build the *ideal* home for our tribe. As we walked, we came across a dagger buried in a thick patch of heather. When I picked it up, the wind blew, the clouds parted, and a burst of glowing dust filled the air. The dagger had summoned magic, in its purest form."

O-kay . . .

"While the magic was active, I pictured the settlement we hoped to build—a castle large enough to welcome as many like minds as the island could hold, fertile land ripe for harvesting, and a generous water supply. As I envisioned each element, it sprang from the earth, fully formed. Valkyris was built in a day, all owing to that singular piece of metal, and the will of the gods."

Holy. Freaking. *Skit.*

"Once the buildings were in place, the gods left us with one final gift—a team of *älva.*"

"Huh?"

"Fairies," Freia said. "From the realm of Alfheim, sister realm to Asgard."

I blinked.

"Asgard, home of the gods," she said slowly.

"Right. I know Asgard." *From the* Thor *movies . . .*

Freia raised a brow, but continued to scale a second flight of stairs. "*Älva* magic powers key elements of our world. Through it, we were able to summon the dragons to our realm. And the *älva* both implement and maintain our more exotic amenities—flameless candles, bucket-less baths, and the like."

Woah.

"To maintain our standing, Valkyris prophets

92

convene daily with the gods—and our patron goddess, Freya. It's important to ensure we conduct ourselves in accordance with the will of our deities. It is through this collaboration that magic remains available to us."

We paused at the top of the second staircase. We were in a serene hallway, with cream-colored stone walls, flameless candle-sconces on the walls, and twin rows of identically carved doors.

"And the dagger?" I pressed. "How did it . . . how did we . . ." I really didn't know how to put this.

Freia paused outside one of the doors. "The *Ting* was approaching, and tensions have been growing. I feared there would be a challenge to Valkyris' dominance, so I went to the sacred ground—the spot where I first found the dagger—and prayed over its blade. I asked the gods to reveal the ideal leader for our tribe— one who would guide us in this ever-changing time, who would enhance my son's strength of character *and* strength of rule, and who would inspire our youth to continue the path Halvar and I established for our people. As I prayed, the dagger disintegrated in my hands—its metal dissolved to the same golden powder I'd seen once before, and it disappeared on a wind. I knew in that instant my prayer had been answered."

"When was this?" I asked.

"A little over two weeks ago."

Yup. Right about the time I'd been minding my business, and came across a time-traveling dagger.

See what early morning exercise gets you, Saga?

"It's strange," Freia mused. "I'd thought the dagger

would lead me to a member of the Valkyris—a girl already trained in our customs, who I could groom for a role in our leadership. But we must need an outsider's perspective to best position ourselves to adapt to the changes happening around us."

"I'm definitely from the outside," I muttered.

Freya clasped my hands in hers. "I am so grateful you were spared the horrors of that wretched tribe. But you haven't told me where you lived before they captured you."

"Well . . ." I hedged. I seemed to have landed in a pretty plum living situation, all things considered, and I didn't want to get kicked out on account of being crazy. But sooner or later, my real origins would come out. And it was probably better if Freia heard it directly from me. "About that. I'm kind of from the area where Clan Bjorn lives, or I was staying there, at least, but I'm not actually from this ti—"

"Oh, there you are, Aunt Freia! I've been looking everywhere for you!" A petite, pixie-like girl with charcoal curls and mocha skin skipped down the hallway. "Ooh, this must be the new girl Erik brought home from the *Ting*."

"How do you know about that?" Freia crossed her arms.

"The whole castle is buzzing about it." The girl rolled her eyes. They were a striking shade—so dark blue, they were practically purple. "What do you think we live in, the Dark Times?"

Almost.

"Helene, I'd like you to meet Saga. You're correct; she *is* our new pupil, and I've placed her in the room beside yours."

"You got the silver suite? Very nice." Helene nodded her approval.

"Thanks." I offered a tentative smile. "It's good to meet you."

"You'll love it here," Helene enthused. "Where'd you come from?"

"Saga was a captive of Clan Bjorn."

Helene gasped at Freia's words. "No! Thank gods Erik saved you!"

It hadn't happened quite like that, but I decided to run with it. "Yes. I'm, uh, very blessed."

Sucked into the past and captured by two Viking clans in two weeks. #SoBlessed

Freia turned to Helene. "I trust you will look after our new guest. I've shown her the layout of the castle, but I'm sure she has questions she'd be more comfortable asking a peer than an old woman."

"Aunt Freia." Helene shook her head. "You're hardly old."

"And that's why you're my favorite niece."

"I'm your *only* niece." Helene giggled, then turned to me. "Has she shown you your suite yet?"

"Not yet." My stomach rumbled.

"You didn't feed her!"

"I asked the kitchen to send two meals up. I trust the two of you can enjoy dinner in the silver suite?"

"Does it still have the window that overlooks the fjord?" Helene questioned.

"We don't make a habit of removing windows," Freia replied.

"Then let's go!" Helene opened the door, and stepped into what I assumed was my room. "Ooh, the linens are *gorgeous* in here!"

"Did you say you were looking for me?" Freia asked.

"Oh. Right." Helene popped her head out. "The bucket-less bath in my suite is only running cold water."

Freia frowned. "That is an issue to be taken up with maintenance."

"*Ja*, but they're going to have to put in a request for an *älva* to fix it. And since *you* have access to the *älva* keepers . . ."

Freia shook her head, a rueful smile tugging at her lips. "Very well. I'll see what I can do."

Helene skipped over to kiss her aunt on the cheek. "Thanks! Now come on, Saga. You *have* to see this suite." The door clicked shut behind her as she trilled, "It's sooooo pretty."

Freia patted my shoulder before walking back toward the stairs. "I'll be in the war room, overseeing our current situation. Send for me if you have any concerns."

"No, I'll be fine." I wasn't about to send for someone in an actual *war room*. "So, I'll see you when . . . at . . ."

Freia offered a kind smile. "Your schedule and a map are on the desk in your suite. My door is always open to you—you're welcome any time, for any reason. Helene will take you to your classes in the morning."

"Okay." I walked to my door, and was about to open it when I glanced over my shoulder. "Oh, and Freia? Thank you. For everything."

The chieftess gave a regal nod before disappearing down the stairs.

I turned back around, placed my hand on the door-knob, and took a deep breath.

Here we go.

CHAPTER 11

THE SILVER SUITE WAS unbelievably spectacular. The door opened into a sitting area, with two blue-and-silver couches facing each other and a mahogany coffee table between them. Farther in, a bay window looked out to the fjord below. Rich, silver velvet curtains framed either side of the window, and a table with four chairs sat directly in front of it. To my right, a step led up to the sleeping area, where a dragon-headed sleigh bed claimed the place of dominance. Plush pillows and a silver-threaded blanket rested at the head and the foot, while a sky-blue duvet cloaked the bed in a fluffy delight. I thanked God, the gods, and those *älva* for whatever magic these Vikings had spun to get their hands on modern bedding.

"Your bucket-less bath is even bigger than mine!" Helene poked her head around a door to the left of the bed. "Come see!"

I stepped toward the bathing room, anticipation fluttering in my stomach. *Did I set my hopes too high?*

When I spotted the enormous, claw-footed bath sitting prominently beside another fjord-view window, I exhaled in relief. "It's beautiful. Wait. Where is the spout?"

"The what?" Helene cocked her head.

"Where does the water come out?"

"Oh." My new neighbor waved her hand. "I don't know. You just say you want to bathe, and it's magically full of hot water. The *älva* do it, I guess."

Not quite what I'd been expecting, but I'd take it.

A rap on the door made me jump. "Who's that?"

"Probably dinner." Helene clapped her hands together. "Aunt Freia said she'd had food sent up."

Oh. Right.

Helene skipped ahead of me and opened the door. She reached out and took two plates from whoever stood on the other side. "Ooh, thanks! These smell great."

The door clicked closed behind her as she crossed to the table in front of the window. "We can eat here, and I'll tell you *all* about the academy."

"Sounds good."

We dug into our plates, my belly rumbling as I alternated between the roasted chicken and rosemary bread. I was about to ask Helene what the other kids here were like when a massive shadow flew past my window.

"What was that?" I blurted.

"I'm not sure." Helene tossed her napkin on the table and jumped to peer out of the window. "Looks like the riders are back. Ooh, and they have the intruders with them."

The riders . . . did that mean Erik was back, too?

"I'd have thought they would have killed them by now. Huh." Helene shrugged.

"Wait, how do you know about the intruders?" Or Freia's execution order?

"It's really hard to keep secrets here," Helene explained.

Oh. *Oh.*

"Good thing I don't have any," I squeaked. God, I was *the worst* liar. I'd better work on that.

Hard.

"Why would they bring them here and risk exposing your location?" I wondered.

"Maybe the interrogator has some kind of plan. I wonder who Aunt Freia sent to question them?"

"It was Erik," I said.

"Busy day." Helene whistled. "Rescue the maiden, interrogate the intruders—I wonder what's next. Maybe he'll finally set a wedding date already."

I choked on a cough. "Erik's getting married?"

"Not according to him." Helene rolled her eyes. "My cousin swears he'll be a bachelor chief, but our laws clearly discourage the rule of an unmarried man. Valkyris is set up for a partnership, plain and simple."

So *that* was why Freia had sent the dagger to kidnap me. Either she was trying to find a way around the laws

100

by surrounding her son with female leaders, or she was hoping that Erik and I . . . that we'd . . .

Another coughing fit overtook me, and I rested my palms on the table while I caught my breath.

"Are you okay? Maybe we should sit back down." Helene placed a hand on my shoulder. "Ooh, never mind! They're torturing the intruders! Want to see?"

"No!" I squeezed my eyes shut.

"Oh, wait. No. They're just questioning them. While the dragons hold them in the water. Ooh, nice move, cousin."

I opened one eye and peeked out the window. Sure enough, two dragons hovered over the sea, an intruder gripped tightly in each of their feet. The dragons flapped fiercely, so their captives' torsos bobbed in and out of the water. A third dragon hovered nearby, an arrow-wielding warrior on its back. Erik stood at the edge of the sea, his back to us. I couldn't make out his words, but I could tell by the tense set of his shoulders that he wasn't thrilled with the situation.

"Can you tell what they're saying?" I leaned closer to the window.

"Erik's probably asking them where they came from, what they were told to do, if they were followed . . . basic interrogation stuff." Helene fingered one of her curls.

"Do you know a lot about interrogations? Ooh." I winced as the archer fired an arrow at one of the men. It struck him in the arm, and his head reared back in pain.

"Just what my cousin tells me." Helene shrugged. "I'm studying to become a healer."

"Really?" The girl eagerly observing what was turning into a public execution was studying healing?

"Yes." Helene raised her chin proudly. "Professor Deja says I have a rare gift for sensing energetic symptoms before they manifest into physical injuries."

"That's . . . really neat." I injected as much enthusiasm as I could into the words. "So is that all you study, or—ugh" I ducked my head as the archer shot again. "I really should not be watching this."

"Erik must have gotten everything he could out of that one," Helene deduced.

"Is he dead?"

"*Ja,*" Helene confirmed. "You can look now. The dragon took him away."

I peeked out the window. Sure enough, now only one intruder hung from dragon feet. I could make out the terror in his eyes, and the cry on his lips. My stomach churned as the archer cocked his bow, and I turned my back to the window. If this was a routine day at the castle, I was going to have to develop a thicker skin.

"Hey." Helene placed her hand on my arm. "Let's go back to eating. I forgot how hard all of this must be for you. Your tribe didn't have dragons."

"No." I shook my head. "My tribe did not have dragons."

"You get used to them." She leaned forward conspiratorially. "They're actually pretty sweet. Especially when they're young. We just got some babies, and they're so cute. Maybe after classes tomorrow, we can pay the Dragehus a visit."

"Maybe." I appreciated the offer. And the chance to see baby dragons definitely piqued my interest. But getting up close and personal with the adult dragons . . .

No, thank you. Ever.

Helene polished off the rest of her dinner, but I could only pick at my meat. My appetite had disappeared.

"So . . ." I hemmed. If I was going to pull this whole Viking thing off, I needed to figure out how to blend in. *Fast.* "My tribe was pretty, uh, removed from this whole world. We were just farmers. We didn't sail, or raid, or interact with anyone, really."

"Really?" Helene tilted her head. "How did you trade?"

"We didn't." I lied. "We were, uh, self-sustaining. So, would you mind teaching me the basics? Stuff everybody else knows here, so I don't embarrass myself tomorrow?"

"Of course!" Helene leaned forward on her elbows. "Do you want to know how things work in our region, or with tribes overseas, or—"

"Everything. I want to know how people live here—how do you make those amazing ships and how do—"

"Surely your tribe had woodworkers?"

"Um, yes . . ." I paused. "But not shipbuilders, per se, on account of our being farmers and all. And speaking of, what do you farm? And what do you do for fun? Just start talking, and I'll take notes on . . . uh . . ."

I looked around for something to write with.

"There should be parchment and writing feathers in there." Helene pointed to the desk near the entry.

Writing feathers.

"Thanks." I retrieved a piece of paper and a feather, then returned to the table. "Okay. Go."

"You need ink." Helene wrinkled her nose. "Were your writing feathers different back home?"

"Very," I muttered. I missed my laptop already. I retrieved a pot of ink and settled back down. "Okay. Now, go."

"Well, for starters, unlike where you're from, most of the tribes around here have seafaring functions. Some are master shipbuilders, some are fishermen, you get the idea. But no matter who they are, in our region trade is a *huge* part of life. While raiding provides a one-time source of riches, it's *trade* that yields a sustainable income—and a solid foundation for future revenue."

"Uh-huh." I scribbled on my paper. "And how do people go about selling things?"

"There are trade routes across the Northern countries leading to towns where craftsmen, merchants, and fishermen can support their families. We even have centers overseas, where people buy pottery, combs, leather goods, and clothing. And our blacksmiths . . ." Helene whistled. "Norse blacksmiths are *the best* at what they do. Our swords, chainmail, and axes are in extremely high demand."

"And you get all these goods to the trade centers by ship?" I scribbled hurriedly on my parchment.

Helene nodded. "Norse shipbuilders make the strongest ships in the world. And our explorers are *really good* at what they do. They chart stars, and follow whale migration routes and bird flight patterns—things that let them know when they've reached a certain region. I'm sure your clan had similar tools as farmers—reading the land so you knew when to plant, harvest, all of that?"

I gave my most convincing nod. "Of course. So, you study nature." I made a note. "And navigation. Ship-building, and fishing."

"And ironworking, farming, clothes making, animal husbandry . . . basically everything we need to survive, we have to produce, grow, or trade for, ourselves."

I was fairly competent back home—an A student, regionally ranked archer, and a halfway decent pie baker, thanks to Mormor's sweet tooth. But here . . . I knew none of those things. How was I going to hide my complete and total ineptitude?

Our lesson was interrupted by a knock on the door. I opened it to find one of the women I'd seen earlier carrying fabric. Now, she stood at the threshold with a neatly folded pile in her hands. "Your trousseau, Miss Saga."

"My . . ." I took the clothing from her. "Is all of this for me?"

"Just a few pieces to get you started," she said kindly. "School clothes, leisure attire, and a few night-gowns. Visit our office as soon as you're able, and we'll measure you for more formal garments."

"Thank you," I murmured. "You have no idea what this means to me."

The woman smiled before scurrying down the hall-way. I carried the pile of clothes to my bed, and blinked the moisture from my eyes.

"I heard nightgown. Do you need help getting out of that dress?" Helene pointed to the thick, blue monstrosity still covering my body.

"I did it by myself last night, but it was pretty hard," I admitted. "If you wouldn't mind, I'll take your help."

"Of course." Helene stepped behind me, and undid my dress.

It slipped easily from my shoulders, and I shimmied into one of the nightdresses before removing the layered skirts from my waist.

"Done. Do you want me to show you how to use the bath?"

"Just explain it to me one more time?"

"Stand in front of the tub and say that you'd like to take a bath. That's it." Helene clapped her hands. "Water appears!"

"Thank you, Helene." I clasped her hands in mine. "I truly appreciate you being here."

"Of course!" She pulled me into a hug. "That's what friends are for! Oh, and I forgot to tell you about after-noon tea—it's offered every day in the main dining hall after classes get out, and once a week on the academy lawn. Celine *always* serves either lefse or waffles. You won't want to miss it."

Seeing as I'd never turned down either of those foods a day in my life, I was inclined to agree.

After Helene left, I took a long, hot, magical bath. I stared out the window, allowing my mind to slow while the water seeped stress from my tired body. I was completely out of my element in every conceivable way, and come morning, I'd face an entirely new set of challenges. But I'd made a friend in Helene, and both Freia and the seamstress had shown me kindness. And Erik . . .

Heat seeped up my neck as I pictured the disarmingly handsome Viking cooking me breakfast. It ebbed as I remembered his seaside interrogation and the subsequent assassinations.

What have I gotten myself into?

After bathing, I dressed in a thick nightgown and settled into the upholstered chair by the window. The flameless candles had flickered on while I'd been in the tub, and I scooted closer to one and studied the notes I'd scribbled while Helene had been talking. The people in this world were so strong, so competent . . . how was I ever going to keep up?

I stood on bare feet and crossed to the desk. Before I slipped the parchment into the drawer, I added one final line to the top. I lifted my . . . *writing feather*, and wrote in my big, loopy scrawl:

How to Viking. By Saga Skånstad.

Someday, I hoped, I'd learn it all.

As I turned away from the desk, a loose piece of parchment caught my eye. My class schedule and the map of Valkyris sat on top of the table—I'd completely forgotten about them in the excitement of magic baths, and public executions, and hot archers, and dragons, and interrogators. My fingertip traced the hand-drawn lines of the map, running from the hills at the edge of the island to the castle in the center, and the sprawl of buildings that bordered the main structure. Their names ran the gamut from Dragehus to domestic barn to church, with one particularly curious structure labeled simply, building. I made a mental note to investigate that one, then turned my attention to my class schedule. Fancy script identified the courses as mine, before detailing the days and hours I was to attend each.

Course Schedule for Saga Skånstad
-Valkyris Academy-

Mandag (Máni's day):
Morning – Inter-Tribal Relations (Professor Idrissen, room 107)
Afternoon – Archery (Professor Sterk, training field)

Tirsdag (Tyr's day):
Morning – Acquisitions and Disseminations (Professor Spry, room 125)
Afternoon –Strategy (Professor Steepleton, room 202)

<u>Onsdag (Odin's day):</u>
Morning – Inter-Tribal Relations (Professor Idrissen, room 107)
Afternoon – Archery (Professor Sterk, training field)

<u>Torsdag (Thor's day):</u>
Morning – Acquisitions and Disseminations (Professor Spry, room 125)
Afternoon – Strategy (Professor Steepleton, room 202)

<u>Fredag (Freya's day):</u>
Morning – Basic Swordsmanship (Professor Greig, outbuilding 2)

My God. I was going to learn all the things after all. So help me, Odin. And Thor. And Tyr. And Freya. And . . . wasn't Máni the personification of the moon?

Sigh.

By the time I climbed into bed, I was completely and totally spent. My heart tugged as I pictured my family, half a world and a thousand years away. Mormor always ended her evenings with one of her crossword puzzles and a cup of mint tea with honey. And my cousin would spend her last waking minutes scrolling through her phone, reading up on the latest environmental issues. I hoped they were doing exactly that—and not worrying too much about me. I was fine. Lonely and exhausted, but fine.

More or less.

It wasn't long before I fell into a deep sleep. The night before, I'd dreamed pleasant dreams of the leather-clad Valkyris heir. But now, my dreams were filled with dragons, death, and the well-aimed arrow of an elegantly lethal assassin. In the scene, I could only see the slender back and long, blond curls of the archer. As the arrow released, the girl swung her hair and glanced over her shoulder with a wink. And I gasped, gripping the bedsheets in terror as I took in her straight nose, high cheekbones, and familiar blue eyes.

The girl who'd murdered the intruder was me.

CHAPTER 12

THE STUDENT DINING HALL was a hive of excitement when Helene and I walked in. She'd met me at my room shortly before breakfast, and woven my hair into the intricate braids she claimed most students favored. She'd left her own curls flowing free, insisting that since combat courses were more loosely structured for healing arts students, she could do what she pleased.

"What's your morning schedule?" Helene took the piece of parchment from my hands as we made our way through the buffet.

"Inter-Tribal Relations in the morning, Archery in the afternoon," I recited.

"Ooh, archery." She returned the parchment, and I slipped it into the pouch at my waist. Since I'd be attending a combat course, I'd selected the tan leggings, white blouse, and blue vest and cloak from my 'starter wardrobe.' The outfit made me feel extremely tough—

like I could take out an entire forest of intruders, steal from the rich, *and* give to the poor, all before lunchtime.

"I'll be in Biology this morning, and Rider Training in the afternoon." Helene placed a selection of bread, fruit, and cheese on her plate. I filled mine with ham, fruit, and . . . ooh, they had lefse!

Too bad Nutella wouldn't be invented for another thousand years.

I followed Helene to a round table, where three girls were huddled together. Their whispers stopped when Helene and I set down our plates.

"Girls, this is Saga. New student; be nice to her." Helene plopped into a seat, and I did the same. "Saga, this is Jules, Tendris, and Audhild. They're in the healing arts program with me."

"Hi." I raised one hand in a nervous wave. Assuming Helene had gone in order, Jules was the redhead, Tendris the one with freckles, and Audhild had the silver combs in her hair.

"*Hei*," the girls chimed in unison. I smiled tentatively and began cutting my ham.

"So." Helene broke off a piece of bread. "What's everybody so excited about?"

"The executions," Tendris whispered. "They've never done them publicly before."

"They've never done them in Valkyris at all!" Jules chimed in.

"I can't imagine what Erik was thinking." Audhild

tossed her hair over her shoulder. "Chieftess Freia must have been furious."

"Unless she ordered it to be done that way." Helene finished her bread and speared a piece of fruit with her knife. *Weird. Where are the forks?* We hadn't had any last night, either. Was there some kind of flatware shortage?

"Why in the world would the chieftess do that?" Tendris asked.

"She was overseeing the whole situation," Helene shrugged. "She must have wanted them to be killed here."

"But why?" Jules rested her chin on her fingertips. "Why would she want us to see something so horrible?"

"Did a lot of people actually see it?" I asked. "Wasn't it done on the side of the castle?"

Audhild raised a white-blond brow. "*Everybody* saw it. There was a music performance scheduled for right afterward—half of Valkyris was already gathered on the lawn."

"Well . . ." Tendris took one last bite, then folded her utensils across her plate. "I think Freia was in on it. The question is, why?"

"Maybe she's trying to send a message?" I copied Helene, and knifed a bite of ham.

"But to whom?" Helene nibbled her cheese. "The men they killed can't report back to their tribes. They're dead."

"True." I laid my utensils across my plate like Tendris had done.

Just then, a deep bell chimed, sending Helene rocketing to her feet.

"Ooh, we'd better get to class. Saga, I'll show you the way." Helene picked up her plate and carried it to a bin near the wall. I did the same, waving at Helene's friends. They waved back, and I hastened out the door and down the staircase. I moved quickly, but Helene stayed well ahead of me, a blur of black hair and blue cape.

When we reached the first floor, she pointed to an open doorway. "Inter-Tribal Relations will be in there. I'll come collect you after class, and we can have lunch together."

"Sounds good," I panted. I was mildly winded from chasing Helene down the stairs. "Boy, your teacher must be a stickler for tardiness."

"Hmm? Oh, right. Yes, I need to be on time, or—oh!" Helene's eyes lit up and she straightened her spine. "Zaan! *Hei!* I completely forgot you'd transferred to morning biology!"

"*Hei*, Helene." A tall, muscular guy carrying a stack of books paused outside one of the doorways. "See you in there."

Helene angled her chest toward the person who was *obviously* her crush. "Absolutely."

I bit back my laugh. When Zaan was safely inside the classroom, I grinned at Helene. "You were saying about a strict teacher . . ."

"Oh, hush." Helene swatted my shoulder. "And *don't* tell my cousin. He'll never let me hear the end of it."

My stomach fluttered at the mention of Erik. "Does he study here too, or . . .?" Did Vikings graduate? God, I had no idea how any of this worked.

"He finished his studies last year, but he helps out with some of the upper division warfare courses. I think he'll be in one of the combat classes this afternoon—I can't remember which one." Helene smoothed her skirt, and tugged the neckline of her blouse down an inch.

Don't giggle, Saga. "Right. Well . . . see you after class?"

"See you then!" Helene pulled her neckline another half-inch lower, then skipped into the biology classroom. Through the open door, I heard her high-pitched squeal. "Zaan! I didn't know we'd be lab partners, too!"

With a smile, I turned and entered my own classroom. Two rows of tables with long, wooden benches faced a podium where a grey-haired, stiff-backed woman stood primly. Bony fingers drummed the surface of the wood, and the stern frown lines between her eyes led me to believe it had been a long time since her last smile. Her eyes settled on me as I hovered in the doorway.

"Miss Saga, I presume?"

Ten heads turned in unison—a veritable firing squad of curiosity.

"Yes, ma'am." I shifted nervously from one foot to the other.

"I am Professor Idrissen. *Velkommen* to my class.

You will sit here." She pointed to an empty seat in the front row.

"Thank you." I ducked into my chair, where a writing feather, ink pot, and piece of parchment were neatly set out. Professor Idrissen walked over and lay a textbook beside me.

"You'll want to read up on the allied tribes—the first two essays in this text detail their leadership and ritual practices, which will be the focus of tomorrow's exam."

Tomorrow? I was a good student, but that was pushing it.

"Now, class." Professor Idrissen returned to the podium. "I'm sure many of you witnessed yesterday's execution of the Clan Bjorn intruders."

So, Lars *had* sent a revenge party after Erik. God, if they'd found him . . . *or me* . . .

"That event marked the first time an intruder has ever breached Valkyris. And do you know *why* Chieftess Freia ordered they be admitted within our borders?" Professor Idrissen scanned up and down the rows.

"To remind us of Valkyris' might?" A freckle-faced guy offered.

"Precisely." Professor Idrissen nodded. "As members of Valkyris, we have the unique position of having been blessed by the gods. And we shall maintain their favor so long as we dwell in the virtues they espouse—love, honor, and loyalty. But there is one among our numbers who has risked not only our way of life, but the favor of our divine benefactors. Someone who accepted payment in exchange for exposing our whereabouts. We do not yet know the identity of this individual, but I assure you, if he or she turns out to be one of my students, the wrath of the gods will be the least of their concerns."

The girl next to me swallowed hard.

"Since we have a new student with us, and this may be a new subject for her, let's take a moment to review what we have learned this term. Who can tell me a bit about the relationships between the allied tribes? Kiersten?"

The girl two seats over raised her chin. "The nine tribes who make up the allies—Valkyris excepted—are among the most brutal in all of the northern countries. They keep women and slaves in positions of subservience, conduct more raids and conquer more lands than any others in the realm, and regularly seek vengeance for blood feuds. Leadership is passed from a chief to his son, or to his nephew if he has only daughters, and citizens are afforded little voice in their own governance."

"Correct." Professor Idrissen's gaze flicked over my shoulder. "Embla, how do the allied tribes maintain peace among their people?"

"They meet bi-annually at the *Ting*—a meeting at which they negotiate the terms of their alliance," a petite girl answered. "Protections are afforded in exchange for goods or slaves"—*or captive brides, if memory serves*—"and oftentimes the tribes will agree to work together to seize a particularly desirable region of land."

"Yes. And what is the function of our people in this uneasy alliance? Finn?" Professor Idrissen pointed to a gangly boy.

He cleared his throat before speaking. "As the allies make up the most aggressive tribes in all of Norway, it is our duty to stand for those who face their oppression. We have successfully converted many tribes to a more progressive way of living, but the allies appear unwilling to evolve. Our role is to maintain the outward appearance of brutality, all the while looking for a way to serve the oppressed. Whether it be through admission to our sister colony on the mainland, Valkyris East, which serves as a decoy for the *true* Valkyris, or perhaps one day through conquering the allies, and imposing our will in the style they best understand—brutality."

"Well put," Professor Idrissen praised. *Still no smile.* "Now, let us continue our discussion of the differing ideals between the allied tribes and the egalitarian society of Valkyris. Finn, you've done well today. You may argue the position of the allies. Kiersten, you may defend Valkyris."

Oh, *skit*. This was a debate class. Or, at least today it was. I'd literally *just* been dropped into this world . . . and I'd *definitely* embarrass myself if I had to argue a position. I sent a silent prayer to any deity that was listening, Norse or otherwise. *Please, please, please don't let me get called on. Kisses, Saga.*

Finn and Kiersten stood and walked to the front of the room. They each folded their hands at their waist, and blinked at Professor Idrissen. I seriously hoped my archery classmates had more personality than this group.

"You each have two minutes. Finn, take the lead." Idrissen nodded.

"Thank you, Professor." Finn drew a breath and faced the class. "In these dark times, we must come together to defend the Norse lifestyle against near-constant threat. Conquerors travel from across the globe seeking to destroy our religion and seize our land. Brutality is the only means by which to preserve our way of life. The allies have remained steadfast in keeping weaker citizens in positions of subservience. Strength is not only its own reward, but the means through which the Norse way of life shall be preserved and disseminated. If the allies were to give in to this egalitarian system of governance, as many northern tribes have already done, we would appear weak in the eyes of our enemies—both domestic and foreign. And weakness *always* begets attack."

Finn nodded at his opponent, who pulled her shoulders back and began.

"While Finn makes an eloquent case, his argument cedes to my position on one key point. Brutality may be a means to preserve a way of life, but does anyone actually want to preserve the allied way of life? They enslave not only neighboring tribes, but their own people, keeping those with less income—and therefore less influence—in positions of powerlessness. Allied women have few political rights, and thus have very little voice in resolving grievances both within their communities, and at the *Ting*. Those tribes the Valkyris have been able to reach—who have embraced the more benign tenants of egalitarianism—have seen a surge in income, productivity, and overall goodwill. It behooves not only the allies, but the greater northern region, to empower women, educate their youth, and allow *all* citizens, regardless of income, a voice in their own governance." Kiersten nodded at Professor Idrissen, who remained stone-faced at her podium.

"Well done," she praised without cracking a smile. "You may both be seated."

Finn and Kiersten returned to their benches, where they picked up their feathers and held them aloft, no doubt ready to take notes.

A barrel of fun, this group was.

"What did you find to be the most engaging points of each argument?" Professor Idrissen pointed to the freckle-faced boy who'd spoken up earlier. "Edvard?"

"Kiersten's argument referenced the tribes Valkyris has already converted to a more advanced way of existence—those who afford women basic rights that range from being permitted to run family properties in their husbands' absence, to being allowed to divorce that husband should he prove unworthy," Edvard responded.

"And Finn's argument . . . Agnetha?"

The girl to my left looked up with a start. She

tapped her fingers on her desk as she spoke. "Finn's argument highlighted the allies' motivation—fear of losing religious freedoms. While Valkyris honors all faiths, many of the conquering invaders seek to usurp our right to worship our gods. The allies are afraid of losing something that matters a great deal to them."

Professor Idrissen nodded. "True. Does anyone believe that empowering those who are currently oppressed would weaken the allies' armies in any way? Saga, what is your opinion?"

My blood stilled in my veins. *Oh, God.* "Me?"

"Do we have any other Sagas in the classroom?" Professor Idrissen pursed her lips.

"Right." I cringed. "Well, I, uh . . . um . . ."

"Oh, dear. Must we enroll you in elocution lessons, as well?"

Snickers erupted from behind me.

Heat crept up my neck, but I forced myself to keep my voice steady as I hurriedly formulated an argument. "Actually, Professor, empowering the oppressed would *strengthen* the allies' position. If their ultimate goal is to defend their land *and* expand their raiding and trading territories, they'll need a continual influx of numbers. Mortality rates for raiders are probably high, so the best means by which they could increase their workforce is to utilize those within their own tribe. Women can run farms, maintain lands, and perform the duties of men while their husbands are away. A structure of this type allows for a greater sense of security, as temporary governance would be placed in the hands of leaders with a vested interest in the tribe's future."

Professor Idrissen looked down her long nose. "Well put. Now, I should like for each of you to fill your parchment with an essay arguing one side or the other. Explain to me why the allies are justified in maintaining their structure, or why they would benefit from empowering their disenfranchised, and converting to a modified Valkyris system of governance. You have half an hour. Begin."

Whew. I exhaled slowly. This was going to be harder than I'd thought. But I picked up my feather and wrote, filling my paper and even turning it in a few minutes *before* Professor Idrissen began her lecture on trade routes.

By the time Helene picked me up for lunch, I was more than ready to get out of that classroom. My schedule had me in archery all afternoon, and I could not wait to go outside and do the one thing Vikings did that I was actually good at.

Maybe I'd even bump into a certain blond-haired heir while I was at it.

CHAPTER 13

ARCHERY WAS INFINITELY MORE enjoyable than Inter-Tribal Relations. The class was held on the lawn outside the castle, where several targets were set up at varying distances. We were to warm up by shooting at the closer targets, move on to the far ones, and finally, shift to the moving bull's-eyes. Our teacher had rigged a series of grain-stuffed bags to swing from the upper branches of a tree, and my three classmates and I spent the better part of an hour shooting just at those. By the time we'd finished, I was exhausted, and exhilarated, and all together happier than I'd been since I'd come here. It was nice to have a piece of familiarity in a completely foreign world.

"Excellent work." Professor Sterk waved us in. My classmates—twin girls with sharp senses of humor, and a guy whose muscles rivaled Erik's—jogged from their targets to stand beside our teacher. I hurriedly retrieved my arrows, and did the same. "You can leave your arrows with me—I'll put them away. I'll have the targets open tomorrow during your free period, so come out and work on your long-range shots if you have the time. That's all for today. Saga, may I have a word?"

"Goodbye," the twins chimed. They placed their arrows on the ground and walked toward the castle arm-in-arm. "See you at dinner!"

"Good work." The guy nodded at me before following the girls.

"Thanks. See you!" I waved at my classmates, grateful they'd been nice. And smiled.

"Saga." Professor Sterk's sparkling green eyes crinkled at the corners as she ran a gloved hand through her short, brown pixie cut. "Archery seems to be a strength of yours. I take it you've practiced before?"

"Um . . ." I'd been Junior Regional Outdoor Champion back home. But since telling Sterk I'd won titles a thousand years in the future would likely earn me a one-way trip to the loony bin, I simply said, "Yes."

Thankfully, Sterk wasn't big on questions. "Good. We're low on archers here, and I'd like to put you on an accelerated course of study. What does the rest of your schedule look like?"

"Oh. Hold on." I set my arrows at my feet, and pulled my schedule from my satchel. "I have Inter-Tribal Relations and Archery on Mondays and Wednesdays, Acquisition and Dissemination, and Strategy on Tuesdays and Thursdays, and Basic Swordsmanship on Friday."

"Just one class on Friday. Are you free in the afternoons?"

I glanced at the schedule again. "It looks like it."

"Wonderful." Professor Sterk scooped up the arrows, and walked toward the castle. I shouldered my bow and followed. "I'd like to work privately with you then, if it's all right? You're very talented, and I believe you'll prove to be of great use to us."

"Thank you." I looked over as we passed an outdoor training ring, where Erik and the archer from yesterday's execution sparred. Since they were shirtless, I had an unobstructed view of two massive sets of shoulders and an impressive array of abdominals. Whatever was in the water here, it had produced a crop of exquisite men.

Stop staring, Saga. It's rude.

In a minute.

Erik lobbed a punch at the archer, who spun out of the way with an easy grin. Erik's smile suggested he was enjoying himself every bit as much as his opponent. Swinging his arm, Erik easily blocked the archer's retaliatory blow, then struck with his leg. He swept the archer's feet out from under him, flattening him on his back and holding a fist in the air. "Winner."

"Two out of three." The archer jumped to his feet and shook his head. "I *will* best you today, Erik Halvarsson."

My pulse quickened. *Erik Halvarsson . . .*

"First time for everything." Erik tightened the wraps around his wrists.

The archer's inky black hair flopped over his forehead, and he swept it back before squaring his shoulders with a smirk. "Let's go."

"Come on, Axel. Do you really want to get your butt handed to you again?"

"Keep dreaming," Axel countered. He launched a jab that landed squarely in the middle of Erik's washboard stomach. He quickly recovered and brought his elbow to Axel's ribs. His hair swung freely over his shoulder as he spun to deliver a roundhouse that left Axel doubled over.

"Want to call it?" Erik offered.

"Not a chance." Axel launched himself at his opponent. The ring was filled with grunts and groans as the two Vikings grappled. Erik forced Axel to the ground and knelt over him, revealing the rivers of sweat trickling between the valleys of eight distinct abdominal muscles. *Holy hell.* How was it possible to look that good?

My insides warmed, and a slow burn had just started to build in my belly when a whisper pulled me from my ogling.

"Saga?" Professor Sterk spoke softly. "May I continue, or would you prefer I leave you here to enjoy the view?"

"What? Oh. Oh!" Heat flooded my neck. I forced my eyes from the sea of sweaty muscles, and shuffled after Professor Sterk's shaking shoulders. "Sorry, Professor."

"I did the same thing when I was your age." She chuckled. "Axel Andersson is one of our top assassins, and one of our few remaining archers. If you won't find him too distracting, I may ask him to oversee your lessons."

"What? Oh, no. I'm not into—" I stopped myself. Sterk thought it was Axel I'd been drooling over. Correcting her would no doubt lead to infinite embarrassment. I pulled my shoulders back, and shook my head. "That'll be fine. I'm sure I can learn a lot from him. And you."

"Wonderful." Professor Sterk paused at the door to the combat wing. "I hope to see you practicing tomorrow."

"You will," I promised. "Thanks for the lesson."

"Of course." Professor Sterk slipped into the castle, and I rested my back against the smooth stones of the exterior. My gaze slid over to the training ring, where Erik and Axel now shook hands. Erik's biceps flexed with the movement, and my heart rate quickened as he turned to give me another view of his absolutely spectacular stomach. I permitted myself one final look at his chest and shoulders before forcing my gaze upward. Our eyes locked for the briefest of moments, during which the heat in my abdomen turned to an absolute inferno. One corner of Erik's mouth quirked in a smirk before I turned my head and hurried into the castle. Inside the prep room I retrieved my Inter-Tribal Relations text, threw my cloak around my shoulders, and headed to the lavender garden on the opposite side of the castle. I needed to cool off, big-time. And a good dose of heavy reading would definitely do the trick.

I hoped.

※

An hour later I sat on a stone bench in the lavender garden, nose deep in the history of the Bjorn-Ragnar conflict. According to my textbook, the two tribes had been at each other's throats for nearly a hundred years, in a dispute that stemmed from a land rights disagreement—as so many did. Half the Viking tribes seemed to have been at odds at one point or another, whether over territory, raid routes, or ownership of slaves. And the internal conflicts . . . I'd read numerous stories of blood feuds that came from thwarted love, overzealous wooing (because that was a thing here), or my personal favorite, long engagements that resulted in pre-marital offspring. *Snort.* The one thing I hadn't seen in my texts was the word, *Viking.* Either it hadn't been invented, or it hadn't made its way into these books. Regardless, I was glad I hadn't spoken it out loud—blending in was already struggle enough.

I'd just traded my Inter-Tribal Relations text for a book on religion, and was intending to read up on Thor, Loki, Heimdall, and the rest of the so-called gods I'd only ever thought of as superheroes, when a deep voice made me jump.

"This seat taken?"

My book landed spine-first on my foot, and I

winced as I bent to retrieve it. As my fingers brushed the leather, a large hand intercepted mine. Warm fingers wrapped around my palm, sending a pulse of heat up my arm and down to my navel.

Gulp.

"Here you go."

My eyes moved past the fingers, up the thick forearms and exquisitely defined biceps of a guy who clearly worked out more than I did. His lightly tanned skin deepened a shade over his massive shoulder, then lightened again across a bare chest that was so spectacularly sculpted, I wondered if it had been the model for one of those ancient pieces from my high school art class. My Lord, those abs were positively awe-inspiring, with eight distinctly defined muscles framed by two diagonal bulges I'd only ever seen on actual movie stars. How was this guy real? Also, why hadn't he put on a shirt after his workout? Was he trying to kill me?

"A little light reading?" Erik's deep tenor forced my eyes to his face, where a strong, square jaw bore a freshly trimmed beard, and endless blue eyes sparkled in the late afternoon sun. God, his eyes really were something. I'd never seen a blue quite that shade. Yesterday, they'd been the clear azure of a summer sky, but today they held just a hint of turquoise—as if a storm cloud had passed through them, and left behind a residual—

"Saga?" Erik questioned. "Are you all right?"

"Huh? Oh. Right. Reading. Yeah." I shook my head.

"Sorry, I was just, uh, really into the . . ." *Abs? Pecs? Arms?* "Book," I finished lamely. "It's a good book."

"Mmm hmm." Erik's pale pink lips pulled upward. He was probably trying not to laugh at me.

"So, what are you doing out here?" I asked politely. It took a tremendous amount of self-control *not* to ogle his chest.

"I'm out of wood in my suite. I like to chop it myself." Erik raised his hand, which I finally noticed now held an axe. A bow hung lightly from two fingers of his other hand, and a quiver of arrows was attached to his belt.

"You planning to shoot the tree first?" I asked.

Erik leveled me with a stare. "Contrary to what my mother would have you believe, threats do lurk within Valkyris."

"I heard." I set the book in my lap and folded my hands over it. "So, there's something rotten in the state of Denmark?"

"What's happening in Denmark?"

Shakespeare hasn't been born yet. Remember?

Oops.

"Nothing. I just mean, there's a spy here? Someone's actually feeding information to the outside world?"

"So it appears." Erik set his axe and bow on the ground, and dropped onto the bench beside me. A faint sweat still covered his bare arms, and I tried not to lean into one as it pressed lightly against me. Or notice how absolutely delicious it smelled.

"What are you going to do about it?" I squeaked.

Erik turned his head. "Are you sure you're all right?"

"Great!" I blurted.

"Uh-huh." Erik brought a hand to his forehead. He ran his fingers through his thick, blond mane with a sigh. "I don't know what we're going to do. This is unprecedented."

"Did the public executions help?" Erik shot me another *look*, and I shrugged. "You did it right outside my window. And Helene was *really* into watching."

"My cousin has a sick sense of fun." Erik rolled his eyes. "And I don't know. We'll watch the borders over the next few days to see if anyone runs."

"Is there anyone you could buy off in Bjorn's camp to sell you information? Someone there *has* to know who the spy is—unless they're passing information via messengers."

"And if they were using messengers, someone in that chain would know the source." Erik stroked the fibers of his beard.

I briefly wondered if they were prickly or soft. *Focus, Saga!*

"Problem is, I don't know who I could trust inside that tribe. It's common knowledge that there's no honor among their clan."

"But there is honor among their slaves." I sat up straighter. "There are two girls trapped there—Ingrid and Vidia. They're good people—I trust them."

Erik folded his arms, and his biceps bulged across his chest.

"What?" I asked.

"I mean no disrespect, but that is an exceedingly gullible statement."

My lips parted in an O. "Excuse me?"

"You've just revealed how little you know about our practices. In Valkyris, ignorance is a liability."

I snapped my jaw shut. "Did you just call me ignorant?"

"Think about it. Slaves—especially Clan Bjorn slaves—are kept in appalling conditions. Conditions most people would do *anything* to escape. Say I were to trust your friends—ask them to help identify our spy. Then what? If they're caught, they'll likely be sentenced to death. And if they *think* they're going to get caught, or if they think there's any chance reporting my offer will earn them their freedom, then they'll inform their superiors—and Valkyris will have another blood feud on our hands."

My teeth ground together. "You have a very low opinion of my friends."

"It's nothing personal. It's the reality of life outside our borders. We can't afford to be soft, Saga. The world depends on us to stop the tide of terror that sails daily from our shores. If we compromise Valkyris, if we place our trust in the hands of people who can be easily bought off, then the entire world will suffer."

I glared at Erik's squared shoulders. "You don't have many friends, do you?"

"I don't need many friends. What I need is to surround myself with people whose strength of character and strength of mind don't get me—or my people —killed."

"You think I'm going to get you killed?" My voice climbed a full decibel.

"I think your lack of awareness is a liability that must be monitored."

Oh no he didn't. "For your information, I am not a liability."

"Saga," Erik said patiently. "I don't know where you came from before Clan Bjorn, but in Valkyris, women are expected to carry their weight. They learn to hunt, fish, fight, craft, and master an academic discipline, all before completing their time at the academy. They're extremely competent. So far as I'm aware, you possess none of those skills. And until you learn, you *are* a liability."

"I am perfectly capable of carrying my weight," I snapped. "And I'm plenty competent, thank you very much."

"Is that so?" Erik said drily.

I shot him a look absolutely loaded with fury. "Hand me your bow," I demanded.

"What are you going to do with a bow?"

I stood. "Just hand it to me."

"Fine." Erik offered up his bow and a fist full of arrows. "Try not to hurt yourself."

Anger roiled within me, but I stamped it down with a growl.

Must not shoot Erik. Must not shoot Erik.

God, I so want to.

"Hay bale, two o'clock," I said. I plucked the weapons from the jerk's hands, nocked an arrow, and pulled back the string. On my release, the arrow whooshed across the lavender garden before landing neatly in a pile of hay. "How's that for competence?" *You Viking jerk!*

"Lucky shot."

Grr.

"Look. I've been here exactly one day, and I've learned the entire history of the Bjorn–Ragnar conflict." I snatched up another arrow and shot. *Bull's-eye.* "I've learned the motivating factors behind the allied tribes resistance to your governance"—I shot again, sinking a third arrow into the hay—"and I've learned the primary trade and raid routes of every tribe in the region." I took one more shot, landing my fourth arrow perfectly. "And what I don't know, I'll figure out as I go. I am *not* a liability. If anything, given the lack of archers in your army and the superior skill I've exhibited since well before I came here, you're lucky to have me."

I shoved the bow into Erik's hands, flung my cloak over my shoulder, and scooped up my books. My boots thundered across the dirt as I stormed from the garden, putting as much distance as possible between me and Erik. I may have been trapped in a foreign world, in a foreign time, but I wasn't about to let some idiot think he was better than me. And I wasn't about to stick around for one minute longer than absolutely necessary. My hands balled into fists as I marched angrily for the castle, my mission clear in my mind.

I was going to find that stupid, time-traveling dagger and wish myself back home if it was the very last thing I did.

CHAPTER 14

"WHOA! SAGA, WHAT'S WRONG? You look so—my gods, what are you doing?"

Helene jumped out of my path as I stormed down the castle hallway. I stopped at the first tapestry I came to, lifted the fabric, and pushed on the stones beneath. When none revealed themselves to be a secret hidey-hole, I moved to the next. And the next. I'd already explored every inch of the walls in three of the four first-floor wings—after the academy wing, I'd move on to the second floor.

"Saga?" Helene pressed.

"I'm finding Freia's dagger," I gritted.

"Her dagger? Why?" Helene scurried after me.

"Because I'm . . ." I bit back the words. *'I'm going to use it to magic myself back to my real life'* was likely to land me in whatever amounted to the padded cell in Viking times. "I just want it," I finished lamely.

"*Ja*, well, so do a lot of people." Helene followed me

to the next tapestry. Dang it, none of those stones hid anything. *Whatever.* I'd check every last inch of this stupid place until I found my ticket out of here.

"Do you have any idea where she keeps it?" The final tapestry was as useless as it's ninety-eight counterparts. It was on to floor two.

"I have no idea." Helene's delicate fingers caught my arm as I stomped toward the stairs. "Saga, what's this about?"

"It's about I want the dagger." I whirled on Helene. "Okay?"

Helene's nostrils flared delicately. "Are you the spy?" she whispered.

"What? No! Why?"

My friend tightened her grip on my arm. "If you're here to steal our relic and turn it over to another tribe, then so help me, Odin, I'll—"

"I'm not a spy!" I threw my hands up, breaking her grip. "I just want to go home!"

"Even after seeing all of this?" Helene gestured to the main door of the academy.

"It's . . . complicated."

The corners of Helene's mouth tugged downward. "I'm sorry you're unhappy here."

"It's not you . . . or the school, or Freia, or any of this. What you're doing here is great, honest. It's just . . ."

Helene placed her hand on my shoulder. "What's going on, Saga?"

"I—it's—" The kindness in her eyes nudged at the

tightly wound ball of anger in my gut. With a heavy sigh, I dropped onto the bottom step. Helene sat beside me and rested her hand on my knee.

"If you really want to go back to Clan Bjorn, I'll find a way to get you there."

"I don't want to go to Bjorn. I was their captive, remember?"

"Right. Ragnar, I mean? I heard you were taken from them."

"I'm not from Ragnar, either." I placed my fingertips to my eyebrows and rubbed at the tension beneath my skin. "I'm from . . . really far away. I got lost and ended up here by mistake. And I think the dagger can help me get home."

Helene's brows shot to her hairline. "How?"

Uh . . . "It's a really special dagger, right?"

"Well, sure." Helene's curls bounced with her nod. "But the gods gifted it to us to grow our civilization. Not to act as some kind of . . . transport for wayward travelers."

She had no freaking idea.

"I get it. I do." I worried my bottom lip. "But if I wanted to track it down, do you have any idea where I could start looking?"

"No. Aunt Freia keeps it locked up somewhere secret." Helene shook her head. "The dagger's sacred— you do know that."

"I gathered," I said drily.

"Freia only brings it out for special events —consecrations, solstice ceremonies . . . she might even bring it to the winter ball if my cousin finally declares his bride."

I was immediately seized by a violent coughing fit.

"So, Erik actually *is—cough, cough—*getting—*cough*—married?"

"Erik was supposed to get married last year." Helene patted my back while I caught my breath. "But he refused to select a wife."

"He's only like, eighteen. Isn't he?"

"Nineteen." Helene's hand stilled on my back. "How old are people when they get married in your tribe?"

Thirty!

"Um . . ."

"In Valkyris, we're married by the time we're nineteen—twenty, tops. It happens much earlier in other tribes, though. Erik's really pushing it, especially considering he's our heir."

Oh, God. I'd be eighteen in a few weeks. If I couldn't find a way out of here . . .

"Where do you think Freia keeps the dagger?" I pleaded. "I *have* to try to get home."

Helene studied me sadly. "I don't want you to leave. I like you."

"I like you too. I just . . ."

"I understand." Helene drew her knees to her chest. "I have no idea where the dagger is. But I seriously doubt it's somewhere anyone could find it. Maybe it's in Freia's family quarters, or in the church?"

Of course! A sacred dagger would be kept in the church. *Duh.* I'd check there as soon as—

"Ladies." A low voice echoed from the staircase. "You're missing dinner."

"Oh, *hei* Axel." Helene looked over her shoulder. She scooted out of the way as the dark-haired Viking jogged down the stairs.

"*Hei*, Helene. And you must be Saga?" Axel held out a hand. His playful green eyes crinkled at the corners as I allowed him to pull me to my feet.

"That's me."

"Axel Andersson. Lead assassin for the Valkyris tribe. I hear you're quite the archer," he offered. "I'm looking forward to our training session on Friday. Sterk wanted to come, but I told her it would be more fun if it was just the two of us."

"Axel." Helene's tone carried more than a hint of warning. "She already hates it here. Don't make it worse."

Heat rushed up my neck. "I don't—"

Axel swore. "What did Erik do?"

"Excuse me?" I asked.

"I saw you talking in the garden. How'd he screw this up already?"

"He didn't—I didn't—what do you mean, *screw this up*?"

"Axel," Helene admonished.

"Oh, come on." Axel raked his fingers through the shock of hair that flopped over his forehead. "Erik rejects every single girl Freia pitches. Then one shows up from out of nowhere. You think we don't all know exactly what's going on here?"

Well, I sure as hell didn't.

"We don't know anything," Helene hissed.

"You may not, Leeney. But I do." Axel stared me down. "He's supposed to be *endearing* himself to you. Not making you miserable. What did the idiot do?"

"I—he—" My brain swam. Erik was supposed to be *endearing himself*? Freia had been pushing girls on him? No way had I been carried across time to marry some backwoods, backwards Viking. No matter how good looking he was.

"Did he hurt you?" Axel crossed his arms. "Because if that idiot laid one finger on you, then I will personally take his ass to the forest and beat him within an inch of his life."

"Freia would kill you," Helene pointed out.

"I'd ask for forgiveness later," Axel growled. "What'd he do, Saga?"

"He didn't touch me," I assured the glowering assassin. "He just called me a name."

Two sets of eyes narrowed.

"What did he call you?" Helene asked.

"He said I was ignorant. And a liability to the tribe."

Axel groaned. "Gods, he is so stupid."

"The stupidest," Helene agreed.

"Of course you're a liability," Axel said. "But why in Odin's name would he tell you that?"

"Wait. What?" I crossed my arms.

"You were taken from a rival tribe," Helene reminded me. "There's a substantial possibility that tribe will come after us in retribution. But that's not your fault. Erik shouldn't have put that on you."

"And he shouldn't have called you ignorant," Axel added. "I heard you held your own against those Inter-Tribal Relations nerds."

"How did you . . .?"

"I told you it's impossible to keep secrets around here," Helene said.

"Yeah. Well . . ." I studied my fingertips. "I'd just rather not be around him."

"Can't say that I blame you." Helene shrugged. "But Erik's really not a bad guy. He's kind, and honorable."

"And one hell of a fighter," Axel chimed in.

"Wonderful," I said drily.

"Aw, don't be like that." Axel cuffed my bicep. "Come on. I'm starving. Which dining hall were you ladies heading to?"

"Saga hasn't eaten in the main hall yet," Helene said. "I thought maybe we could go there."

"Great." Axel threw an arm around my shoulders, and guided me away from the academy doors. "Celine promised me she'd make mutton stew tonight. It's my absolute favorite."

Mutton? Wasn't that . . .

"Sheep stew?" I swallowed my distaste. "Sounds great."

"Don't worry," Helene whispered as she stepped beside me. "She always makes a vegetarian option, too. I can't stand mutton."

I shot Helene a grateful look as the six-and-a-half

foot Viking beside us all but skipped toward the dining hall. After dinner, I'd go straight to the church and hunt down that dagger. Then I'd be on the first trip out of here.

God, I hoped this worked.

CHAPTER 15

THE MAIN DINING HALL was considerably fancier than its academy counterpart. Not only were the tables set with linen napkins and what appeared to be legit silverware, but they were etched with ornate, mythological carvings that ranged from Thor's hammer to an eight-legged horse to a massive, fanged wolf. And every single female gracing the long rows of tables had dressed for dinner.

Every female but one.

I skulked between Axel and Helene, neither of whom had mentioned the dress code, and wished fervently that I'd changed out of my training clothes. I didn't own anything formal, but even the apron-dress the seamstresses had gifted me would have been better than the leggings, belted tunic, and cape I was currently rocking. Despite my attempt to channel invisibility, more than a few women looked up in disapproval as I slunk onto one of the polished benches at a corner table.

Way to make a first impression, Saga. Nailed it.

I averted all eye contact as I unfolded my napkin, set it across my lap, and filled each of our glasses with water from a nearby pitcher. Axel settled on the bench to my left, and Helene slid in across from us. They both looked up with easy smiles as a server carried a full tray to our table.

"We eat as a family here. Others will probably join us shortly," Helene explained as the server unloaded a plate of vegetables, a loaf of crusty bread, and a tureen filled with what had to be the mutton stew. Brown chunks of meat floated among peas and carrots in a thick broth.

"And for you, Miss Helene." The server set a plate of cheese and bread in the center of the table before whispering, "I know how you feel about the mutton."

"Gods bless you, Thyra." Helene placed a hand to her heart. "This is my new friend, Saga. She'll be sharing the cheese platters with me on mutton night, if she knows what's good for her."

"Hey," Axel protested. "I love this stew."

"Lucky you. You get the whole bowl to yourself." Helene smirked.

"*Hei, hei*, Saga. It's lovely to meet you." Thyra offered a friendly smile. "If there's anything else you need, just let me know."

"Thanks. I really appreciate it." I glanced down at

145

my plate. "Oh, do you have an extra fork? I seem to be missing mine."

"Fork?" Thyra tilted her head.

"You know, like . . ." I looked to Axel's plate, but his fork was missing too. And Helene's. I picked up my spoon. "Like this, but pointy?"

Helene shot me a curious glance. "We don't have pointy spoons here. Was that something you used in your old tribe?"

I snuck a glance at the table across from ours. Sure enough, its occupants stabbed chunks of mutton with their knives—no pointy spoons in sight.

Good Lord. I'd wandered into a world where forks hadn't been invented yet. Either that, or they hadn't made their way to Vikingdom. *Bizarre.*

"Uh . . . yeah." I set my spoon down. "Sorry, my mistake."

"Valkyris must seem very strange to a newcomer," Thyra said kindly.

She had no idea.

"*Ja*, but Saga's starting off strong." Axel slung his arm around my shoulder. "She landed *me* for her archery tutor. Somebody's having a lucky week."

I rolled my eyes good-naturedly. "I never said I needed a tutor. Only that we could shoot together."

"You wound me, Saga." Axel's eyes pulled downward in feigned sorrow. "Most girls would kill for alone time with me."

I swatted his arm away with a laugh. "I think you'll find I'm not most girls."

146

"That you're not." Axel sighed. "You'd appreciate me, wouldn't you, Thyra? Or would you crush my heart, too?"

From the way Thyra's cheeks pinked, I had a fairly good idea of her answer.

"Axel! Sorry about him." Helene turned to Thyra. "I swear, we can't take him anywhere."

"It's quite all right. Just wave if you need anything else." Thyra picked up the tray and scuttled off, the pink now stretching all the way across her ears.

"You're awful." Helene shook her head at Axel, who crossed his hands behind his head and leaned back.

"You love me," Axel grinned.

Helene's sigh could have been heard across the room. "Axel suffers from what we in the healing arts like to call 'delusions of grandeur.'"

"I have no idea what that means," Axel said happily.

"It means you have a more-than-healthy amount of self-confidence." Helene smirked.

"That I do." Axel winked. "After all, I *am* descended from gods."

"Excuse me?" I choked on my water.

"That is unequivocally not true." Helene sighed. "You have to stop telling people that."

"It *is* true, and I'll tell who I please, thank you very much," Axel said. "It's well known in the Andersson family that some Asgardian somewhere blessed our lineage with a touch of the divine."

"Keep telling yourself that." Helene chuckled.

"Oh, I will, Leeney. I most definitely will."

"Axel! There you are!" I looked up from doling out cheese to find two girls racing across the dining hall. They practically tripped over each other in their haste to claim the empty seat next to Axel. I was pretty sure I saw at least one thrown elbow.

"*Hei* there!" The taller of the two reached our table first. She slid gleefully onto the bench, adjusting her low-cut dress for maximum cleavage.

Snort.

"Birna." Axel nodded. "Brigga. How are things?"

The busty girl's doppelganger frowned as she took the seat across from Axel. She leaned forward on her elbows, optimizing the view of her own chest, and pushing Helene out of the way in the process.

"Hey!" Helene objected.

Brigga shot Helene a catty look before turning her attention to Axel. "We didn't see you in the Dragehus." She pouted. "We waited all afternoon."

"I had other business to attend to." Axel winked. "Nice of you ladies to keep an eye out for me, though."

So, Axel was *that* guy—the one all the girls fought over. I guessed there was one in every era.

"Axel," Birna purred, "if you're not busy tomorrow, I'd love to get your advice on training. I'm getting one of the babies as my dragon charge, and you're *the best* at managing them."

Axel nodded. "It's all about working out the power dynamic. Establishing your dominance"—the girls burst into giggles at the word. *Seriously?*—"but keeping your animal happy by letting it *think* it's in control."

"I'd love for you to show me how to assert my . . . dominance." Birna batted her eyelashes, earning an award-winning eyeroll from Helene.

"Gods, Birna, does that ever actually work for you?" Helene pushed Brigga so she was once again in front of her own plate.

Brigga and Birna shot Helene twin glares.

"Well, *Helene*, I don't see you with any marriage offers. Guess that great big brain of yours isn't worth so much after all," Birna snarked.

Axel raised his hands. "Stand down, Birna."

"Come on, Axel. She's *obviously*—"

"She's *obviously* my friend. And nobody talks to my friends like that."

Birna flinched at Axel's angry tone.

Brigga jumped to her sister's defense. "She only meant—"

"I know what she meant. And I won't tolerate *anyone* talking to my friends like that. Ever."

"She started it," Birna muttered.

I shifted uncomfortably in my seat. The table suddenly felt very small.

"It's true. Helene's had it in for us since we started spending time with Axel." Brigga twirled her hair around one finger. "Think it's a coincidence that we were downgraded to a double room last month? She used her influence with her precious 'Aunt Freia' to make sure we—"

"Enough." Axel groaned, interrupting her. "Brigga, Birna, find someplace else to sit. I don't have the patience for your drama tonight." Axel angled his shoulders to me. "Saga, will you pass me the stew?"

Birna's eyes widened before narrowing into slits. "Saga, is it?"

"Mmm hmm." I slid the tureen to Axel, and resumed selecting cheeses. The brown one was new to me— probably another sheep product.

"Are you the girl Erik brought home?" Brigga asked. I briefly wondered if these two had a thing for Erik, too.

Of course they do, Saga. He's hot.

No, he's not. He's a jerk.

"Um . . ." I shifted nervously in my seat.

"Great. Now you've made both of my friends uncomfortable." Axel eyed the girls coolly. "Get out of here, now. I mean it."

Brigga and Birna's faces clouded over. They fired matching hate-filled glares at me and Helene before stalking across the dining hall and sidling up to a guy-filled table. They were clearly on the hunt.

Jeez.

"Now, where were we?" Axel knifed a piece of mutton and took a vigorous bite.

"You didn't have to do that," Helene murmured. "I can handle Birna."

"You're my friend, Leeney." Axel shrugged.

"*Ja.*" Helene smiled. "But now who will *entertain* you in the Dragehus?"

"Please," Axel scoffed. "Do you really think they were my only source of entertainment?"

I choked on my cheese. "Excuse me?"

"In case you hadn't noticed, assassins are fairly desirable around here." Axel patted my back until I stopped coughing. "Especially the highly good-looking ones."

Helene sighed. "Like I said. Delusions of grandeur."

"Like I said. Descended from gods." Axel grinned at Helene before returning his attention to his stew. "Have you been to the Dragehus yet, Saga?"

"Uh . . . no." And I wasn't entirely sure that I wanted to.

"I'll take you over after our shoot around on Friday," Axel declared. "Helene, how's that Horned Greenwing you're taking care of?"

"His tail spike seems to be healing." Helene sipped her water. "But if he keeps fighting with his stall-mate, I'm going to have to separate them permanently."

"Wait until springtime." Axel chuckled. "Last year, he got into a massive dominance match with one of the other juveniles. Ended with a chunk of somebody's back sitting on the stall floor. I can't remember whose."

"Excellent." Helene groaned.

"You'll break him," Axel promised. "His last trainer was useless, but you've got the knack for it."

"Wait. I thought you were a healer?" I asked.

"I am," Helene said. "But training is a core component of the healing program. We have to be able to coerce the animals in our care into letting us look after them. It's fairly easy with the cows and sheep—and humans, for that matter—but dragons require a bit more finesse."

I could only imagine.

"It's only one term of actual training and another term of riding. Anything beyond that and we call in the riders to wrangle them. Every good healer knows it pays to have friends who can manage the more . . . unmanageable animals." Helene nodded at Axel. "Why do you think I put up with this guy?"

"Because I am a delight," Axel retorted. "Obviously."

"Obviously." I smiled.

Axel tucked into his food, and I grinned at Helene before doing the same. For the first time since I'd gotten here, I felt just a little bit at home.

And for that, I was a lot bit grateful.

CHAPTER 16

AFTER DINNER, I HEADED to the rose garden under the guise of "clearing my mind." I waited until I was sure Helene and Axel hadn't followed me, then snuck around the castle, past the domestic animal barn, and made my way to the church.

I'd expected to find the wooden structure empty, but as I crept along the shoreline that bordered the craftsman's buildings I noticed light streaming from the open windows, and voices carrying across the evening air. Some kind of event was happening inside the church—whether a service or a meeting, I couldn't tell. Whatever it was, it was seriously going to interfere with my dagger-finding plans.

I ducked behind a birch tree that was close enough to the church's open door that I could eavesdrop. A lyrical, male voice recited what seemed to be a prayer to the old gods—I caught the name Odin more than once, along with . . . who was Tyr again? The God of Winter. No, the God of War.

Whoever was in there was praying about a war!

I inched closer before dropping to my knees to stay out of view. I knelt in the grass below the window, and angled my head up to hear better.

"Protect us, great War God, patron of warriors, in these, our final days of peace." Hold on. I'd heard that voice before. *But where?* "Our prophets have seen a battle that will mark the end of a great tribe of the north. Watch over us, Tyr, and ensure our strength brings honor to the gods."

Several voices murmured their agreement before reciting a prayer. The service must have broken up after that, because hushed conversation quickly filled the church.

"I don't know why we couldn't do this in the open," a bitter-sounding male spoke first. "How are the gods supposed to hear us through these walls?"

"Our citizens know nothing of what the prophets have seen," a familiar voice countered. "As leaders, it is our duty not to cause them more worry than absolutely necessary. If that means meeting indoors, then that is what we shall do."

Hold on. Was that Erik?

"Erik is right." A woman confirmed my suspicions. Which meant she must be . . . *Freia?* "Our dealings here must be kept in confidence. If we are to go to war, we will give our people time to prepare. But until we are absolutely positive, we will carry on as if all is well."

"But the prophets have seen it. War *is* coming."

"We cannot know that for certain," Freia countered. "Our prophets have seen a battle that will mark the end of *a* tribe—not *our* tribe. They have not determined the scope of the battle, or even confirmed that Valkyris will be involved."

"Valkyris is *always* involved," the male spat. "And yet we do not seize control of weaker tribes. Our numbers should grow by the thousands, and yet we restrict ourselves to an island."

"Watch your tone, Raynor," Erik growled. "Your chieftess is *not* to be undermined."

"My *chieftess*," Raynor spoke the word as a curse, "refuses to act in the best interest of her tribe."

"On the contrary," Freia said calmly. "What I *refuse* is to risk the security of the one seafaring settlement in all of Norway that honors the values of the gods. Our neighbors may bring terror and death on their serpent-headed ships, but Valkyris will *always* bring honor and knowledge. We will *always* stand for equality among *all* —regardless of sex, or origin, or status as free or thrall."

"Again with the thralls," Raynor said angrily. "You're well aware that slaves would increase our productivity tenfold. At least allow us to use them on our mainland settlement. If we are to go to war, we need all the blacksmiths and warriors we can get."

"No," Erik said firmly. "Valkyris does not practice slavery."

"Not yet," Raynor countered.

"So long as Freia and Halvar rule this island, we

shall *never* force a human into servitude. And when I rule, things will be no different." Erik's angry growl sent a wave of goose bumps across my neck.

"Then maybe it's time for a change in leadership."

The tension was so thick, I was positive Erik and Raynor—whoever he was—were about to throttle each other. Or worse, if Viking church etiquette allowed them to pack weapons. But about the time I expected to hear the sound of shattered teeth or broken bones, a third male voice carried through the window.

"That's enough. Raynor, you have overstepped your bounds. Apologize to my wife."

"Halvar," Freia murmured.

Erik's dad! That's who'd been saying the prayer. I hadn't realized he'd returned home.

"It's important that—"

"Enough!" Halvar bellowed. "You clearly do not agree with our way of life. Perhaps it is time you find other accommodations."

"Are you *banishing* me?" Raynor balked.

"If your banishment is in the best interest of the tribe, it shall be ordered." Halvar spoke with deadly calm.

"I am sorry, *Chieftess*. I'm sure you know what's best for our people." Raynor's tone made it clear he believed no such thing.

God, who was this guy?

A long silence followed Raynor's apology, during which I desperately wanted to peek my nose over the windowsill to see who'd murdered whom. But after a seeming eternity, Freia's voice pierced the quiet.

"You are on notice, Raynor. One more threat to Valkyris, and I will have no choice but to relocate you."

Boots stomped angrily on wood, and I pressed myself against the building as a tall, lanky man stormed out of the church. He bent down to pick up a good-sized rock, which he hurtled angrily into the ocean before marching on the Dragehus.

"Perhaps I should go after him," Freia murmured.

Yes. Go after the angry Viking who just ran to the dragons. Please, somebody do that.

"He needs his space," Halvar said. "I will speak with him in the morning."

"Halvar, I—"

"Come, my love. It is late. Erik, are you returning to the castle?"

"I'm going to take a ride," Erik said.

"Son, I think you should—"

"I won't be long. I just need to clear my head."

It was a big night for head-clearing.

"Very well. We shall see you at breakfast."

The sound of kisses was followed by light footsteps. I pressed myself against the building just as Freia and Halvar emerged. They paused as an enormous, green dragon rose from the Dragehus with a single rider on its back. The reptile roared, a fireball rolling from its mouth and descending on the ocean, before it took to the skies and soared out of sight.

Seriously, nobody thought they should stop that?

"He'll be all right." Halvar kissed the top of his wife's head.

"I wish he were happy here." Freia linked her arm through Halvar's, and continued toward the castle.

"So do I, my love. So do I."

As Halvar and Freia neared the castle, I bit down on my bottom lip. Maybe I should follow them.

Or maybe, since a crazy stranger had just taken off on a fire-breathing carnivore, I should work my butt off to find that dagger so I could *get the hell out of here.*

Survival prevailed.

Erik took his sweet time leaving the church. I stood outside for another two minutes, easy, before his glorious, broad-shouldered form sauntered out of the building. I held my breath as he took the same path as Raynor, walking past the shore and angling in toward the Dragehus. Moments later, he emerged atop a red-scaled reptile, whose glowing eyes and fierce presence quickened my heart rate. Erik let out a cry and the dragon ran for the sea, lifting up just as its toes skimmed the water's surface. It lapped Valkyris in a slow circle while Erik scanned the ground. My breath hitched as he passed over me, still standing outside the church window with my fisted hands and clenched jaw. Our eyes locked, and the glimmer of a shadow passed over Erik's face. His lips turned downward, and I wondered if he was about to ground his dragon and let me have it.

But instead of touching down, he pulled the reins up, driving the dragon higher into the sky, and steering it away from Valkyris. He kept his gaze locked on me until he crested the nearest mountain and disappeared from view.

I didn't realize I'd been holding my breath until dizziness overtook me. I leaned against the building for support, sucking in massive gulps of air.

What the hell just happened?

I dropped my elbows to my knees and bent over, breathing slowly until I was fairly confident I could walk without stumbling. I made my way into the church, too overwhelmed to fully appreciate the carved marbling on the central pillars, or the way the late-evening light danced through the tiny openings in the top level of the structure. The only things I could think about were my intense need to locate the one piece of weaponry that could serve as my ticket out of here . . . and the image of Erik riding a dragon through the sky, his golden hair streaming over bulging shoulders as he—

Stop it. Focus on the dagger. No matter how magnificent Erik looks.

Right.

I paced the wooden building, testing floorboards to see if they doubled as hiding spaces. Then I moved on to the walls, the benches along the sides, and the columns. Everything was solidly constructed, but then I hadn't expected the dagger to be hidden in plain sight. It was probably near the altar . . . or maybe in the pulpit?

I hurried to the front of the church, where I ran my

hands along the table, up and down the podium, and along the back panels. My fingertips traced the carvings of runes and ancient gods, but none of them revealed a trap door or hidden panel of any kind.

Dang it. The church was a bust. Maybe it was hidden in the ceiling?

I craned my neck. The structure had a small base, but it was easily three stories tall. And so far as I knew, the building was sorely lacking in ladders. There was no way I was getting any higher than my five feet, seven inches. If the dagger was up there, I sure as hell couldn't get to it.

Unless there was a smallish dragon I could ride . . .

You're going to bring a fire-breathing animal into a wooden building? Also, you think you can ride a dragon?

Point, brain.

Defeated, I slunk out of the church and plopped down on the grass. If I couldn't figure this out, there was a very real possibility I might never see my family again. And that was a reality I refused to accept. *Think, Saga.* I'd thought for sure the dagger would be inside. Helene had said it was sacred, and what was more sacred than a church, for God's sake? Where else could it possibly be?

Maybe on the grounds?

I jumped to my feet and raced around the building, looking for freshly dug dirt, a cleverly concealed box . . . anything that might lead me to my ticket home. After two laps, the only lead I had was a fresh bed of fire-weeds. I tore into the earth beneath the fuchsia blooms, digging until my fingertips were raw. When I finally sat back on my heels in defeat, the daylight had nearly gone, and the moon was rising over the mountain. All I had to show for my efforts were ten dirt-caked fingers, a bevy of displaced flowers, and an infinite amount of unfettered frustration.

My fingers fisted around the grass, and I ripped two chunks from the earth before flinging them as hard as I could. What the hell was I supposed to do now?

Heaviness wrapped around me as I re-planted the fireweeds, smoothed the hole I'd created, and trudged back to the castle. Darkness had descended once again, and I was no closer to going home than I had been yesterday. Or the day before that. Or the day before that.

I had no idea where to go from here.

CHAPTER 17

THE NEXT MORNING, I was awakened by a battalion of sunbeams streaming through wide-open drapes. In my disappointment, I must have forgotten to close the curtains. *Perfect.* I pulled my comforter over my head, willing time to stop for just ten more minutes. The thought of facing a castle full of cheerful Vikings, all of whom actually belonged here, was more than I could fathom in my exhaustion coma. Especially considering this place didn't even serve coffee.

A pert knock on the door forced the covers from my head. "What?"

"Saga, it's me—Helene. Are you coming to breakfast?"

Skit. I must have overslept.

"I'll meet you there," I yelled back.

"Hurry! Thursday is waffle day!"

Well, that was good news. Not only did I live for

waffles, I doubly lived for Thursdays. They were the official Friday eve. If I was lucky, this place shut down on weekends and I could sleep clear till Sunday.

With a sigh, I rolled out of bed. I cleaned up, and dressed in one of my new apron dresses—a cream under-gown with a blue top layer. I hurriedly wove my hair into braids, and peeked out of my window. The sun bounced brilliantly off the ocean, illuminating the training ring where two shirtless guys were already battling it out. Today's weapon of choice was the broadsword, and I allowed myself one moment of staring at twin sets of impressively toned backs. God, the guys around here were built like—

My heart pounded in my chest as the guys lowered their swords and looked up at the castle. The dark-haired one pointed, and the blonde shielded the sun from his eyes . . . *and looked right at me.*

Oh, God. It was Erik. And he'd caught me staring. Again.

Erik's training partner waved enthusiastically, and I raised my fingers in a tentative greeting. Axel's face broke into a grin, and he punched Erik in the shoulder before twirling his sword and stepping back into the ring. Erik studied me for another moment, his expression incomprehensible, before turning around and stalking toward his friend. He raised his sword, the muscles in his back flexing with the movement, and I took one more moment to appreciate the way the sun glinted off each of the defined bulges. If there was no coffee, I was going to take whatever stimulant I could get.

Helene was gone by the time I got to the student dining hall, so I grabbed a waffle to go and ate it while I jogged down the stairs. When I got to the first floor, I checked my class schedule. Acquisition and Dissemination—A&D, for short—in room 107. Which was . . . I walked down the hallway until I reached a room with two long tables, each filled with pages of documents. More papers sat in bins along a countertop, and a handful of students rifled through books on a shelf by the window.

"Saga, I presume?" A friendly looking woman smiled from the front of the room. With her jet-black braids and creamy, olive skin, she didn't look a day over twenty. Was she a student, or . . .? "Welcome to A&D. I'm Professor Spry. Come in. Let me explain how things work here."

I crossed to the teacher, ignoring the curious stares piercing me from the tables. I got it. I was new. *Get over it, already.*

"We train disseminators here—the people responsible for acquiring and disseminating information throughout the northern countries." Professor Spry pointed to the parchment-filled bins. "Tribes are required to document the findings of their expeditions, and provide a copy of this report to Valkyris. We catalogue each new object or piece of information here, then pass these condensed reports on to the disseminators upstairs. Our post-graduate counterparts assimilate annual reports in bound volumes"—she pointed to the books on the shelf—"and deliver them to regional leaders, who then make them available to their citizens. This way, the discoveries explorers bring home are available to all."

"So *that's* what you do in here." Relief washed over me. "I was afraid the 'acquisitions' part was going to be, uh, pillaging."

And I'd never raided anything besides the fridge, so . . .

"Contrary to allied opinion, the greatest treasure our explorers bring home is not gold, or silver, or *thralls*." Professor Spry spoke the word with a frown. "It's knowledge. The northern countries are fairly isolated from the rest of the world. Our harsh winters and remote locale make us an undesirable port for most traders. Were it not for our explorers, we would have little knowledge of the world beyond ourselves. But thanks to our superior shipbuilders, and the brave men and women who voyage across the seas, we are able to collect information from civilizations across the world, and disseminate that information throughout our own society."

"Freia said something about that," I remembered. I just hadn't realized she was running the medieval equivalent of the internet. Which would make these A&D students . . . the tech nerds.

Snort.

"We work in teams, so I'm going to put you with my niece, Katrin. She and her partner are cataloguing a voyage that just came in from the south. I believe this ship sailed to Rome, and may have stopped in a North African port, as well."

I nodded. "Just show me what to do, and I'll—"

My blood chilled as Professor Spry walked me over to a workspace where a slightly younger version of herself sat with the cow I'd met at dinner. The one who'd thrown herself at Axel, and openly mocked Helene.

"Brigga? Katrin? This is Saga. She's going to be joining your team."

The black-haired girl looked up with a friendly smile, but Brigga's emerald eyes narrowed as she sized me up.

"Saga, is it?" Brigga cooed. "Don't worry, Professor. We'll take *good* care of her." The words positively dripped with insincerity.

"Wonderful. I'll leave you to it." Professor Spry moved on to a team by the window, while I kept a steady eye on Brigga. Rule number one of dealing with mean girls: never let them see you sweat.

"Saga, why don't you itemize *this* list." Brigga shoved a piece of parchment at me. "I'll keep working on the Roman shipment."

"You've been trying to decipher that list all week. She's not going to understand it on her first day." Katrin shook her head. "I'll work on it with you, Saga. Do you want to move to the outdoor space? Professor Spry puts tea and lefse out there."

"Sure. Thanks." I arched an eyebrow at Brigga, and

followed Katrin through a doorway in the far corner of the classroom. We stepped onto a veranda, where two groups were clustered around circular tables. Snacks stood on a smaller table near the lawn, where more students were sprawled, reading textbooks and chatting quietly.

"I prefer it out here." Katrin grabbed two writing feathers and a pot of ink from what appeared to be a supply table. "Will you bring over some lefse?"

"Of course." I placed two pieces of the flatbread and generous dollops of cinnamon-butter onto two plates and carried them to the spot Katrin had claimed. She'd smoothed out the parchment, and was studying it carefully. "So, what do we do?"

"Usually we itemize the acquisitions, and cross-check to confirm similar products or information hasn't already been documented for that region. But in this case, we don't understand what the reporting explorer is talking about. I've never heard of a berry that stimulates fits of energy."

"A berry that . . . wait, what?" I leaned over the parchment.

Katrin pointed to a scribbled line. The writing was so smudged, it was barely legible. "This says a shepherd observed his goats exhibiting bursts of energy after eating a berry. Or maybe it's a bean, it's really hard to read."

An energy-giving bean. Please, God, let this be coffee!

"According to the explorer, another account of the

berry—or bean, I can't tell—came from the East. There they cook it into a drink, which they consume in anticipation of . . . late-night worship services?" Katrin shook her head. "Is it a new kind of tea? I've never heard of a tea bean. Berry. Ugh."

"It's coffee!" I blurted. "Those explorers found coffee! Did they bring any back?"

Katrin squinted at the parchment. "It looks like they tasted the berries, and confirmed the stimulating effects, but were unable to bring any home."

Nooooooo!

"Where did this ship come from?" I panted.

"Northern Africa," Katrin said. "I'm sure another voyage will return from there within the next year or two. Maybe they'll bring this . . . coffa?"

"Coffee." I spoke the word as if it were a prayer.

Katrin tilted her head. "How do you know about it?"

Skit. Right.

"We, uh, had it in my old tribe. Once. A traveler brought it through and he, um, traded it for a few weeks' lodging."

"Hmm. Well, was it good?"

"It's the greatest beverage in the history of ever," I breathed. "Way better than that awful tea."

Katrin frowned. "You don't like our tea?"

"It's too bitter for me." I wrinkled my nose.

"Well, of course it's bitter. It's tea. Did you try adding honey?"

"It's less bad with honey," I admitted. "But coffee . . .

Hey, do we have any kind of sway here? Can we tell the explorers where to go, or what to look for?"

Katrin covered her smile with her fingertips. "You really want that berry. The good news is that at the end of the term, Professor Spry compiles a list of the newly discovered items she believes will be of the greatest use, and recommends the disseminators encourage explorers to pursue further acquisition of those things. The bad news is, the explorers rarely listen to us."

"Really?" My heart fell.

"Really. They're motivated by the financial payoff of more desirable items, like gold and thralls."

"Slaves?"

"Yes," Katrin said. "And those who aren't fiscally motivated are driven by the need to explore and conquer—they're not so interested in serving the greater good."

So . . . there would be no coffee. Not any time soon, at least. "Oh."

"But on the plus side, we cracked this list. That's huge for us. Brigga's been staring at it for days, with no result." Katrin inched closer. "Between you and me, she's not exactly the brightest."

"I gathered." I leaned over the list, and studied another line. "Does that say . . . eating instrument from Rome?"

"It does. Oops, this must have been logged into the wrong manifest." Katrin picked up a piece of lefse and popped it into her mouth.

I stared at the wobbly script. "*Multi-pronged* eating

instrument?"

"We don't have those here." Katrin stared at the lawn. "I wonder if it's some kind of a spoon that was broken, or—"

"A fork! It was a fork!"

Katrin's brows shot to her forehead. "Let me guess: you had those in your old tribe, too?"

"We did! We didn't have to spear things with knives, and risk cutting our tongues or anything. We just took the fork and . . ." I mimed stabbing the waffle, and lifting it to my mouth. "It was all very dignified," I summarized.

"Neat!" Katrin studied the parchment. "And it looks like they did recover several . . . forks, did you call them?"

"Yes."

"So, we should be able to procure a drawing, or a sample, and hopefully our craftsmen can create a few prototypes."

I shot Katrin a grin. "So, this is what A&D does— brings the best of the outside world into Norway."

"And Sweden, and Denmark," she confirmed. "The information we acquire, we share."

"And the northern countries grow and develop because of it. This is extremely cool. Uh, neat," I amended, when Katrin shot me a curious glance.

"It really is. Disseminators are able to contribute to the greater good without lifting a sword or riding a dragon. For those of us who are less adventure-inclined, it's a positive way to make a difference."

"I like that." I bit into my lefse as Brigga walked by the window. The glare she shot me was outright menacing. *Yikes.* "What's Brigga's deal? She doesn't seem as into all of this as you are."

"She's not," Katrin confirmed. "She wanted to be a rider like her sister, but she went berserk out on her first day and got kicked out of the program."

My jaw dropped. "What happened?"

Katrin leaned closer. "Apparently, she had a thing for one of the instructors. Brigga didn't like the way one of the other students was looking at him, and she loosened the girl's saddle when she wasn't looking. The poor thing didn't know until she was a hundred feet up, and her saddle slipped right off."

"My Lord, was she okay?"

"One of the instructors was flying nearby and he caught her, thank gods." Katrin shuddered. "Otherwise, she'd have been dead for sure. If I were you, I'd steer clear of Brigga."

"Duly noted." *Great.* I'd been here all of a few days, and I'd managed to get on the bad side of a homicidal Viking chick.

"What do you think?" Katrin asked. "Should we call it a day or try to decipher another item from this list?"

"Let's keep at it." Who knew? Maybe we'd discover chai lattes next. And maybe if I found an in with whoever oversaw the explorers, I could find a way to bring coffee to Valkyris.

God willing, it would be my parting gift.

CHAPTER 18

DESPITE PERFORMING REASONABLY WELL in the rest of my Viking Academy classes, and even with my years of archery training, Basic Swordsmanship was proving to be a bust.

There were ten students in the class, eight of whom were first years who literally swung circles around Katrin and me. My new friend had flunked three times, and if she didn't pass this round she wouldn't be allowed to graduate in the spring. I was just trying not to embarrass myself in front of the teaching assistant— one infuriatingly demanding and unfairly attractive Erik Halvarsson.

Not only was Erik pretty much the prince of Valkyris, but he was the alumni tasked with guest-teaching the indoor introductory class in what was apparently his very best subject. Professor Grieg had introduced him as "the finest swordsman the academy has ever produced," and Erik's insanely muscular chest had puffed at the praise. Now he was demonstrating an advanced move to the first-year pair on my right, both of whom had it practically mastered.

Show-offs.

"Saga. Katrin." Erik's deep tenor rang in my ear. "Why don't the two of you walk through the sequence?"

I turned my head, and was met with a set of pecs straining against the fibers of a fitted tunic. *Don't stare, Saga. And for God's sake, do not drool!*

"You can keep helping those guys." I angled my sword at the first-years. "We're fine."

"You are not fine." Erik moved closer, wrapping his hands around mine and adjusting my grip. "Who taught you to hold a sword?"

I'd never held a sword a day in my life. A fact I'd explained earlier under the guise of *my tribe was a peaceful farm village.* Obviously, Erik had a listening problem.

"Your wrist needs to be firm." Erik's grip tightened around my forearm, his arm muscles flexing with the movement. *Yum. No, not yum. Grr.* "If your wrist is limp, you're going to injure yourself. We went over this at the beginning of class."

"Yeah, well, it's hard." This sword was freaking heavy. It easily outweighed my bow by a couple of pounds.

"Life's hard. Hold the sword correctly." Erik shifted his attention to my partner, and I used every bit of my willpower to not kick him in the shins.

"You've improved, Katrin," Erik praised. "Your grip is solid, your angles set. If you're able to execute the sequence, I see no reason you can't move on to the next set of steps. I think this is going to be your year."

"Gods, I hope so." Katrin stuck out her bottom lip and blew a stray strand of hair from her face. "My parents will never let me hear the end of it if I flunk out of the academy for poor swordsmanship."

"That would be unfortunate." Erik turned to me. "Katrin's parents are warriors."

Ouch.

I practiced the swing we were working on, turning my wrist inward at the last second. "I can't believe they'll fail you if you don't pass one class."

"I told you, everyone here is expected to carry their weight." Erik watched as I repeated the swing. "That includes being able to adequately defend our borders. And ourselves."

"Yeah, well not everyone's a natural swords . . . swordsperson." I swung again, earning a frown from Erik.

"Still wrong. The wrist should turn out, not in. Like this." Erik lifted his own sword and demonstrated.

"Fine. Better?" I swung again. At this point, I'd repeated the motion so many times my biceps were shaking.

"Not better. Saga, you're not even trying."

"I am too trying!" I exploded. "There are just a lot of things to think about."

"Then think about them." Erik sheathed his sword

and counted off on his fingers. "Grip, wrist, angle, swing. And the sequence couldn't be simpler. Cut to the right shoulder, cut to the left shoulder, duck, overhead, retreat."

I'd show Mr. Perfect a cut to the right shoulder all right. *And quite possibly, one to the neck.*

"Do it with me." Erik unsheathed his sword and held it aloft. Katrin backed quickly away. "Right shoulder."

By now, everyone was watching. *Awesome.*

"Erik," I hissed.

"Do it," he ordered.

Screw my shaking shoulders. I was not about to be humiliated in front of a group of freshmen.

I raised my sword and brought it around in a clockwise swing. Erik's block sent a fierce vibration traveling up my already-sore arm. *Ouch.*

"Left shoulder."

I swung again, counter-clockwise, and was met with another bone-rocking block. *Why does this have to hurt so much?*

"Duck," Erik barked. His sword came barreling at my face, and my knees buckled, dropping me onto my butt.

"Ow!"

"Get up. We'll go again." Erik held out his palm. I glared as I gripped it, and pulled myself up.

"Fine. Right shoulder." I swung as I spoke, bending my knees to absorb the impact of the massive blade. "Left shoulder." I swung again, harder this time.

"Duck," Erik warned. "Overhead."

I brought my sword behind my head and arced it downward. The clang of metal on metal was practically deafening, and I held tight to my weapon's hilt to keep from toppling forward.

"That's better. Again. Right shoulder," Erik ordered.

"We just did this!"

"You think an enemy is only going to attack once? You, of all people, should know the importance of being able to protect yourself."

Oh, he *so* did not go there.

"Right shoulder." He nudged my sword with his.

I swung, channeling all of my frustration into the movement. I'd never have admitted it, but Erik was right—I *did* want to be able to defend myself. Because one day, hopefully soon, I was going to get the hell out of here. And nothing would stand between me and my old life. Not some brutish Viking tribe. Not some arrogant heir. *Nothing.*

"Better. Now left shoulder. Duck. Overhead. Good, again. Right shoulder."

With each cycle, my movements grew steadier. Stronger. Fiercer. By the end of the class, every muscle in my body trembled with exhaustion. But I'd earned a tight head nod from Erik, and Professor Grieg's approval to begin the next series of steps.

"Good luck," Erik offered as he sheathed his sword. "Something tells me you'll be needing it."

I glared at him. "You planning another round of torture for next week?"

"This was a one-time visit. Contrary to what you may think, I have better things to do than teach basic maneuvers to first-years and remedial students. No offense, Katrin."

"None taken." My friend hung her sword on the wall with a smile.

I narrowed my eyes. "Helene said you taught combat."

"I *assist* with upper-division classes. If you work your way up to fourth year swordsmanship, you may have the pleasure of another lesson. Until then." Erik turned on his heel and stalked from the room, leaving me gaping at his retreating back.

"Could he *be* any more arrogant?" I whirled on Katrin. "God, what is his problem with me?"

"You heard him." Katrin shrugged. "He wants you to be able to protect yourself. He wants that for all of us."

Maybe. But . . . "Why does he have to be such a jerk about it?"

Katrin's brows knitted together. "I guess because he knows what it's like to lose someone he loves. And to know that if he'd been there, it might have ended differently."

Wait. What?

"Well done today, ladies." Professor Grieg interrupted the question I'd been about to voice. *Who did Erik lose?*

"Thank you, sir." Katrin turned to our teacher. "I *really* don't want to flunk this year."

"You've been one of my favorite students three

years running." Professor Grieg's eyes crinkled at the corners. "It will be a shame for me to let you go."

"Go?" Katrin wrung her fingertips together before whispering, "You're kicking me out?"

"I'm kicking both of you out." Professor Grieg's coffee-colored eyes bored into mine. *Gulp.* "I'm moving you to my second-year class. Do well next week, and you may even be at grade-level by the end of the term."

"Yes!" Katrin leapt into the air. "Thank you! We won't let you down."

"I trust that you won't." The teacher smiled before hanging the remaining swords on the wall. "Now go on, girls. I hear Celine is serving salmon for lunch today."

"Ooh, salmon is my favorite," Katrin practically purred. "Come on, Saga. And after lunch I'm going to find my parents and tell them I am not a failure. You hear that, world?" She tilted her head back and shouted to the ceiling. "I. Am. Not. A. Failure!"

She practically skipped from the room, leaving me to follow in her wake. While I was happy for my friend, I couldn't quite bury the questions she'd planted in my mind.

Who did Erik lose? And why does he blame himself?

CHAPTER 19

THAT AFTERNOON, I CHANGED into a fresh pair of training clothes, and headed to the weapons room to retrieve a bow and arrow. I selected a mid-sized version before making my way to the green. Axel was already there, loosing arrows on the warm-up targets he'd set at varying distances. Another, equally large guy was with him. His back was to me, but judging from the lean lines of his waist, and the cascade of blond waves falling over thick shoulders, I had a pretty good guess as to who'd crashed my shooting practice.

And I was none too pleased about it.

"Erik," I muttered as I took my place in front of a target.

"Saga," he replied, loosing an arrow and hitting the bullseye at what seemed like a near-impossible distance.

Ugh.

"I thought this was a private party." I cocked my brow at Axel.

"It was, but Erik's a *wretched* shot. If anybody needs my tutelage, it's this oaf."

"He doesn't look like a wretched shot." I placed the hand not clutching my bow on one hip. "Why is he really here?"

The assassin huffed. "I am a benevolent, judicious assister of all. Especially grown men with questionable aim. I take offense to your implied accusation."

"Axel," I warned.

"Okay, fine. I look out for my friends, and I don't like that Erik insulted you. I told him he had to come and make things right."

I turned to Erik. "Is this true?"

"Partly." He fired another shot, striking another target in the center. *Double ugh.* "He told me you were upset, and I *chose* to come and set things straight. I did not mean to offend you, Saga. And I apologize for having done so."

"Oh. Well." My boot toed the grass. "Thank you."

"But I stand by my assertion that entrusting thralls with privileged information is a risk."

"Erik!" Axel groaned.

"It's a risk," Erik reiterated. "But we take calculated risks all the time. For example, I chose to befriend Axel, even though I knew his arrogance would eventually irritate me to madness."

"Hey!" Axel frowned.

I covered my smile with my fingertips.

"And I chose to retrieve you from Clan Bjorn, even though I knew it could lead to a blood feud. My mother was adamant that you would contribute to our society, and she has never led us wrong. Not yet, at any rate."

I wasn't sure whether to thank him or punch him.

"My point is, I am open to hearing your proposal regarding your thrall friends."

"Ingrid and Vidia." I gritted my teeth. "They have names."

"Right."

"They do," I ground out. "And you'd be lucky to have them on your side. God, you're so dim."

I fired off a series of shots. I nailed each of the targets Axel had set, then marched forward to retrieve my arrows.

Erik's footsteps padded right behind me. He reached over my shoulder to collect one of his own arrows, and his bare arm brushed against my shoulder. A spark shot through me at the contact, creating a slow burn that ebbed from my shoulder all the way down my torso. Erik stepped closer, driving the heat lower. The pulse below my navel weakened my resolve, and I found myself leaning into his intoxicating nearness. The scent of pine and sweat wafted from the expanse of bare skin along his arms, and I permitted myself the slightest of swoons before forcing myself to rip my own arrow from the target.

"Then enlighten me," Erik murmured.

"Huh?"

"You think I'm so dim? Enlighten me."

Oh. Right. My friends' virtue. *Defend, Saga. Defend!*

I forced myself to summon the indignation I'd felt before my Erik-sniffing. "Well for your information, Ingrid and Vidia are extremely loyal. And extremely smart. Lots of slaves die in Clan Bjorn, whether from abuse or during attempted escapes." The girls had told me as much. "But they've kept their sanity by forging a friendship. They encourage each other when things get hard, and that bond is the reason they've made it as long as they have. If you gave them a reason to fight, and to fight together, I have every confidence they would rise to the challenge."

"Perhaps." Erik moved on to the next target, and removed his arrow. "But what's to keep them from selling me out? Inciting a blood feud?"

"What could they possibly have to gain from that?" I plucked my own arrow, and pushed past Erik. "Clan Bjorn's never going to offer them their freedom. But if you did . . . they'd do anything to get out of there. Of that, I'm one hundred percent certain."

"You have that much faith? In women you knew for just . . . how long were you Bjorn's captive?"

I ripped my arrow from the final target and whirled on Erik. "You don't need a lifetime to know someone's heart."

Erik's eyes softened, and he moved to stand right beside me. He shifted forward, and my pulse quickened at the realization of what was about to happen.

My God, he's going to kiss me! Do I want him to kiss me?

Who am I kidding? Of course I want him to, but should I let him kiss me? Do people even date here, or does a kiss mean something more? Oh no, if he kisses me does that mean we'll be—

My thought-spiral came to a grinding halt as Erik placed one hand on my shoulder, guided me gently to the side, and reached past me to remove his arrow from the target I'd been blocking. Then he stepped backward with a nod.

Oh. Right.

There would be no kissing. Not that I'd wanted any.

Yes, you did.

Oh my God, SHUT UP!

"If it means that much to you, I will reach out to your friends about assisting us. If it ends in a blood feud, so be it. We're due for a war, anyway." Worry lines framed Erik's eyes, and I wondered if he was thinking about whatever prophecy he'd been discussing in the church. Before I could ask, he turned on one heel and stalked back to Axel.

"You make it better?" Axel called out.

"Ask her." Erik jabbed his thumb over his shoulder. His butt flexed beneath tight leather pants as he walked.

Down, girl.

"We're good," I confirmed. I forced my eyes away from Erik's butt, and jogged back to the shooting line. "Erik's going to offer my friends refuge in Valkyris in exchange for information about the spy."

"Were those my terms?" Erik arched a brow.

"They were mine," I retorted. "And once Ingrid and Vidia out the perpetrator, you can thank me properly."

Erik's eyes twinkled. "And what would a proper thanking look like to you? Mmm?"

"I'll come up with something." I waved a hand. "Just get them out of there, sooner than later. It's hell on earth where they are."

"So I hear," Axel muttered. "Erik, why don't you go write up the terms? I've got some things I want to show Saga this afternoon, but I can leave to contact the thralls and relay our instructions in the next few days."

"Excellent." Erik nodded. "Axel. Saga."

So formal.

"Erik." I nodded back.

When Erik had disappeared into the castle, Axel turned to me with a grin. "Good. He's gone. Now the real fun begins."

I crossed my arms. "You're not planning to ambush me with more stubborn males? Got any other irritating friends who want to crash?"

"Oh, I have *plenty* of irritating friends," Axel confirmed. "But none coming to ride with us."

"Ride? I thought we were shooting."

"We are." Axel's grin stretched from ear to ear. "But a little birdie told me you don't know how to shoot on dragon-back."

All blood promptly drained from my face. *On dragon-back?*

"Calm down. I'm not starting you on the carnivores." Axel chuckled. "You have to work your way up to that. You ever ridden a horse before?"

"Uh . . . does being forced to flee the *Ting* on Erik's horse count?"

"Okay, correction. Have you ever ridden a horse by yourself before?"

"Not well."

"Well then. The first lesson will start in the barn. I'll teach you how to command an animal: get it to do what you want it to. After that, we'll move on to shooting in motion. And once you're comfortable *there*, we'll graduate to dragons."

"Great," I squawked.

"Don't worry, Saga. I'm an *excellent* teacher." Axel patted my shoulder before strolling across the field. He glanced back with a cheeky grin. "What are you waiting for? Barn's this way!"

Right. I gripped my bow and marched confidently after Axel. I could do this. I *would* do this.

God, I hoped I didn't get eaten by a dragon.

CHAPTER 20

THE NEXT MORNING, I woke up sore. Not 'I ran an extra mile in gym class' sore, but 'my God, I've been pummeled by a heavyweight boxer and trampled by an elephant' sore. I'd thought my trip to Valkyris had been uncomfortable, but my time on Erik's horse had been a walk in the park compared to my time on Cyril—a juvenile male with infinite energy. The stable hand swore he'd assigned me one of the gentler animals, but I wasn't so sure. Cyril's tail had twitched the minute I'd entered his stall, and I could have sworn there was a mischievous twinkle in his eye as I crawled awkwardly onto his back. Axel had insisted I ride bareback—apparently, saddles as I knew them weren't so common here—and it was with absolutely zero grace that I slid from Cyril's shoulders to his haunches in a vain attempt to steady myself. Things got mildly better once Axel showed me how to grip with my knees and heels, and doubly better once he bridled old Cyril and let me hold tight to the reins. But two hours into Horse Riding 101, I was chafed, raw, and totally exhausted.

And we hadn't even started the target practice yet.

By hour three, I'd managed to trot a short distance with my hands on my head, and by hour four I could hit a target while cantering. But I'd also fallen off Cyril four times, nearly impaled myself on my bow twice, and had almost sprained my ankle on a particularly unfortunate dismount. Needless to say, Axel decided to hold off on the dragons.

Thank God.

I'd intended to lounge in bed all weekend, but in my injured and exhausted state, I'd forgotten to shut my curtains—*again.* Since the sun here was every bit as hearty as the Vikings it shone upon, it beamed relentlessly until I dragged my aching body from my bed and squinted out the window. Below, the lawn was filled with early risers doing every imaginable form of activity—wrestling, sword fighting, axe throwing . . . A handful of kids were even tossing around a disc. Nearby, people were spread out on blankets, picnicking and playing what looked like some kind of chess game, while clusters of tiny boats rowed up and down the shore.

Good Lord, did these people never rest?

A knock on my door pulled me away from the window. I opened it to find the seamstress I'd met on my first day here, carrying another pile of clothing. Her eyes widened as she looked over my wrinkled nightdress and sleep-addled face. No doubt my bedhead was something to be feared.

"Morning," I offered sheepishly.

"Good morning, Miss Saga. I hope I didn't wake you."

"Not at all. I'm so sorry; I don't know your name."

The woman smiled kindly. "I'm Magda."

"It's nice to *officially* meet you, Magda." I smiled back. "Come on in."

"I'm just here to drop these off." Magda offered me the pile, and I took it.

"Thank you," I whispered. "You didn't have to—"

"We wanted to. We noticed you've been spending a lot of time engaged in physical activities, so we made you some extra sets of sporting attire. There's also a swimming outfit in there—I'm not sure if you know, but on weekends here, we like to engage in a multitude of sporting competitions."

"Ah. So that's what's happening on the lawn."

Magda nodded. "The events begin at dawn, and go on all day."

Saturday Saga had a very different idea of fun to her Valkyris counterparts. "You're not an idle people, are you?"

"That we are not." Magda smiled. "Now, if you'll excuse me, I'm off to join the revelry. Will I see you outside?"

"I'm not sure. But thank you." I clutched my new clothes to my chest. "This means a lot to me."

Magda's eyes crinkled in a smile. "It is truly our pleasure, Miss Saga. Enjoy your morning."

With that, she scurried down the stairs, leaving me with a brand-new pile of clothing. I crossed to my bed, and carefully set out each piece. There were pants, blouses, and vests for shooting, and a pair of leggings with reinforced knees—those must have been for riding. *Gulp.* Two more apron dresses and under gowns, an old-timey onesie—that must have been the 'swimming outfit,' *ha!*—and . . .

My lips parted in a low whistle as I unfolded the most elaborate ball gown I'd ever seen. It was made of a delicate blue fabric that was chiffon-like in texture, but shimmered in the light as if it had been crafted by a bevy of fairies. It had a deep *V*-neck and thick straps that hung off the shoulders, and its narrow waist flared at the hips to create a voluminous skirt that flowed all the way to the ground. It was the most spectacular piece of clothing I'd ever received.

I immediately wanted to try it on.

"Saga!" a perky voice called from the hallway. "It's me, Helene! Are you going to stay in there all day?"

"I'm strongly considering it," I called back. But I opened the door, and let my friend in. "Hey."

"Saga! You're still in your nightgown? It's already eight o'clock!"

I didn't bother explaining that where I came from, on a Saturday, that was pretty much dawn.

"Ooh, did the seamstresses make you more outfits?" Helene skipped to my bed, and ran her fingers along the shimmering blue fabric of the gown. "Oh, my gods, is this for the winter ball?"

"Maybe?" *Drat.* I'd been hoping it was an 'every Tuesday' kind of dress.

"You're going to freeze in this. I hope they made you a cloak. Or—oh. My. Gods."

"What?"

"It's heated! The *älva* must have enchanted it!"

Crazy morning-person Viking said what?

"I don't understand." I moved closer to Helene, and fingered the gown. "How can a dress be heated?"

"How can our baths instantly fill with hot water?" Helene shrugged. "But stick your hand under the skirts. Go on!"

I slipped my hand beneath the fabric and sure enough, a gentle warmth coated my skin. It ebbed up my arm and down my torso, stretching all the way to my toes until my entire body was a comfortably toasty temperature.

"Whoa," I whispered.

"I've never had an *älva*-enchanted gown before. The seamstresses must really like you." Helene beamed. "Now get dressed. We're missing the footraces!"

I ducked my head in embarrassment. "Listen, Helene, I'm really not up for . . . all of that." I gestured to the window.

"Oh. Okay. Do you want to stay in? I can teach you to do some of the more complicated braids on yourself."

"No. I don't want to keep you from the fun. Get out there." I smiled. "I'll see you at lunch, or maybe dinner."

Helene furrowed her brow. "Are you sure?"

"Go." I shooed her away. "I'll come find you when I'm ready to jump into weekend life. I promise."

Helene reluctantly backed out of my room, promising to check on me later in case I changed my mind. The second she left, I crawled back into bed and pulled the covers all the way up to my nose. I was achy, exhausted, and overwhelmed.

And I was homesick.

Now that I finally had a minute to myself in a place where I wasn't scared for my life, or trying to convince an entire tribe I was just the average Viking next door, I could open the hermetically sealed door in my heart and process the pain of being separated from my family. I hoped Olivia was happy at NMU, working toward her Environmental Studies degree and pledging our moms' beloved sorority for the both of us. And I wondered what Mormor, the rest of my cousins, and my aunt and uncle were doing right then. Hopefully they weren't going out of their minds worrying about me. I was safe, and completely unharmed, physically. But emotionally . . .

I was out of my element in every conceivable way. I missed my home, my family and my world. I was mentally exhausted from hiding who I really was, and physically exhausted from the insane schedule everyone else seemed to think was business as usual.

And for reasons that defied all logic, I couldn't stop thinking about the world's most irritating Viking heir.

I'd never been a hotter mess in my life. And I had no idea how I was ever going to feel normal again.

❄

I missed my family terribly during the next three weeks. My classes were intense, nearly every waking moment filled with training and debating and learning *all the things*. My shooting skills had already improved just from the few classes I'd had with Professor Sterk and the practice hours I'd logged on my own. I was less awkward with a sword than I'd been when I showed up, though it would never feel as natural in my hands as a bow. And I'd settled into an easy routine, eating meals with Helene, Katrin, and their friends, and asking just enough questions to figure out how to fit into a world I still knew relatively little about. My learning curve was steep, but I was managing.

With Axel off to Clan Bjorn, I didn't have to ride any horses—or dragons, thank God—for the time being. But that didn't mean my days were easy. There were swords to wield, and strategies to learn, and of course, I regularly attended the academic inquisition that was Inter-Tribal Relations. I collapsed on my bed most nights completely exhausted, but nobody around me ever seemed to tire. I couldn't fathom how they maintained this level of energy *all the freaking time*. By

Friday afternoons, I was done—I needed two full days just to recover.

I managed three blissful weekends within the comfort of my room. But on the fourth Saturday, a pert knock sounded on my door. Helene was back. And this time, she wasn't taking no for an answer.

"Aunt Freia said I had to give you space, so I did. But darn it, Saga, you're missing the best part of living on Valkyris! We have so much fun out there. *Please*, won't you just join us already?"

My weekend solitude was making me stand out for all the wrong reasons. With a sigh, I gave in to Helene's violet puppy-dog eyes. "Fine. I'll come."

"You will?" Helene clapped her hands together. "Yay!"

"So, uh, what should I wear to sports day?"

"Hmm? Oh, for *leikar*?" Helene glanced down at her own outfit—an apron dress in a pretty green shade. "Depends on what you want to do, I suppose. Do you plan to row? Swim? Try your hand at swords? Play *hnefatafl*?"

"Excuse me?"

"It's a board game where you try to capture as many of your opponent's figures as you can, without losing many of your own," Helene explained.

"Oh. Chess!"

Helene raised a brow.

"We had a game like that in my tribe—we called it chess," I hastened. "And, uh . . . I like swimming. Sword fighting, not so much."

"Fair enough." Helene marched over to my wardrobe and picked up the swimming outfit the seamstresses had made me. "Put this under one of your everyday dresses. A roomy one, so you can join in the footraces if you want to."

"Perfect. Thanks, Helene."

"Any time." She skipped to the door. "I'll grab some leftover lefse for us while you change. Meet me downstairs when you're done?"

"Sounds good."

I quickly slipped into my clothes and washed up, then joined Helene on the first floor. I took the offered lefse and followed her onto the lawn. "I can't believe you guys actually do this every Saturday."

"And Sunday, after morning worship," she said. "We take our sporting days very seriously."

She wasn't kidding. Grunts and groans came from the arena, where swords clashed, wrestlers grappled, and kids ran laps around the ring. Shouts rang from the water—the cheers of rowers racing their long boats along the shore. And on the field, a group of men were lining up with thick, wooden bats.

"What are they doing?" I pointed to the bat-bearers.

"Ooh, good. We didn't miss the *knattleikr*."

"The what?" I'd never get used to these names. Apparently my internal translator had some glitches.

"They didn't have that in your tribe either?" Helene tilted her head. "Come on, let's go watch. You'll pick it up eventually."

I followed Helene to the edge of the field where we

joined a group of women sitting on the grass. We plucked a blanket from a pile and laid it out. I'd just dropped to my knees and was adjusting my skirt beneath me when Helene let out a squeal. "Ooh! Zaan's playing! Look!"

Sure enough, Helene's crush lined up with seven other shirtless guys. They each carried a wooden bat, which they thumped menacingly, while a team of nine squared off opposite them.

"We're down one." Zaan looked up from his thumping. "Where's Erik?"

"Here. Sorry, I'm late. Dragon problem." A bare-chested Erik jogged from the direction of the Drage-hus. Did he never wear a shirt?

Are you actually complaining?

Point, brain.

I tried not to drool as Erik bent down to scoop up a bat, affording me a view of the taut muscles of his back, and the tight curves of his butt. *Mmm . . .*

"You okay?" Helene whispered in my ear. "You're panting."

"No I'm not!" I elbowed her in the side. "Just watch the game."

"Whatever you say." Helene tucked her knees beneath her.

"Axel not coming again?" one of the guys asked.

"He had to take off for a while," Erik replied. Flutters filled my stomach as I thought about Axel, who was still on his mission to help Ingrid and Vidia. God willing, they'd get him the information we needed about the spy and would be coming to live with us soon.

"Are we going to play or what?" A thick-browed guy slapped his bat against his hand.

A grin lit up Erik's face. "Pitch the ball, Mathias."

"I thought you'd never ask." Mathias threw what looked like a woolen ball high into the air. Erik swung, connecting with the ball and launching it to the far end of the field. All eighteen players charged after it, punching, kicking, and tripping one another in their haste to claim the prize.

Good Lord, they were going to kill each other.

Zaan was the first to reach the ball. He scooped it up, turned around, and charged back down the field. He used his bat to deflect the advances of Mathias' teammates, at one point thwacking an opponent so hard the poor guy dropped to his knees and wept.

"Is he okay?" I whispered.

"He's fine." Helene rolled her eyes. "He's just a baby."

"I don't know." I winced as three guys swarmed Zaan, thwacking him with their sticks until he fumbled the ball. "That looks *really* painful."

Helene shot me a sideways look. "Of course it is. How else would they get him to release the ball?"

Clearly, organized Viking sport failed to observe the modern convention of fouls.

Or referees.

The game continued for well over an hour. Points were scored when someone managed to run the ball into what amounted to their end zone. Zaan was the fastest runner, while Erik and Mathias proved to be the biggest bruisers of the bunch. Erik's well-aimed blows took out half of Mathias' teammates. They limped to the sidelines when they'd had enough, clutching bloody shoulders, wounded ribs, and in one case, what looked to be a sprained wrist. *Ouch*. When only Erik and Mathias were left on the field, the two grinned menacingly at each other.

"Yield now, and save your remaining teeth," Erik taunted.

"And deny myself the pleasure of beating you senseless?" Mathias threw his head back with a laugh. "Never."

"Have it your way." Erik threw the ball in the air. The two men swung, their bats connecting with such force that a deafening *crack* echoed across the field.

"Uh-oh," Helene murmured. "That's not good."

"What's not good?"

"Splintered bats mean somebody's going to get impaled."

What?

Sure enough, the ball went flying down the field with two Vikings chasing after it. When Erik scooped it up and charged toward his goal, Mathias chased after him with his broken stick. Only this time, instead of bludgeoning Erik with its side, Mathias rammed his opponent's shoulder with the jagged edge of the wood. Erik threw himself out of the way at the last second, leaping into his end zone with a pained cry. As he jumped, he swung his foot around in a fierce arc. His heel connected with Mathias' jaw, launching him flat onto his back. The ensuing *thud* was practically deafening.

"I yield," Mathias mumbled.

Erik climbed to his feet with a triumphant grin.

A second later, he dropped to his knees and groaned.

"He's bleeding!" I gasped at the trail of blood coursing from Erik's shoulder. "Badly!"

I jumped up, but Helene gripped the hem of my dress, holding me in place. "Don't. You'll embarrass him."

"He needs to put pressure on the wound. Are there medics here, or advanced level healers, or—"

"Saga." Helene tugged me back to the ground. "They do this every weekend—and worse during battles. My cousin knows how to take care of an injury."

I worried my bottom lip as Erik limped toward his teammates. One offered a piece of cloth, which Erik wrapped tightly around his shoulder. He turned to Zaan, who secured the cloth in a tight knot before murmuring what I hoped was solid medical advice.

"Zaan's in your healing class, right?" I hissed at Helene.

"He is." She smiled. "Don't worry, Saga. Your man will be fine."

"Erik's not my—" I broke off at Helene's self-satisfied smirk.

"Whatever you say."

"He's not! In fact, I think he's—"

"Saga." Erik's low tenor interrupted what was about to be one epic denial. "I didn't know you enjoyed *knattleikr*."

I looked up—and up—to see the massive, blond behemoth. His bare chest was covered in cuts and bruises, and blood had seeped heavily through the cloth at his shoulder. But he was standing, smiling, and appeared to be in reasonably good health.

For someone who'd been pummeled by sticks.

"It's my first match," I admitted. "I'm not sure it's my favorite sport."

"Me either." Erik grimaced.

"*Hei*, cousin." Helene drawled. "I thought Mathias was finally going to take you on that one."

"Please," Erik said. "Mathias can barely walk. Look at him."

I glanced to the field, where two of Mathias' teammates helped him to his feet. They supported his weight as he limped to the sidelines, clutching his cheek. Zaan jogged across the field, and spoke quietly to the injured player.

"Is he okay?" I whispered.

"He may have dislocated his jaw." Helene shrugged. "Zaan will check him out, and set it if necessary. We always have a few healers around on sporting days."

"Right." There was nothing else I could say.

Helene nudged me with an elbow before blinking up at her cousin. "And speaking of healers, Erik?"

"Hmm?"

"Why don't you and Saga take a little swim? The

saltwater would be good for cleaning out your wound. Just put a fresh bandage on it afterward."

Wait. What?

"I hardly think Saga wants to swim," Erik demurred.

"She has her swimming outfit on under her dress," Helene countered. "And she said she loves swimming. *Loves* it."

"I said no such thing!" Though it was true. I'd missed my early morning swims since I'd been sucked into Vikingdom.

"But you did put your swimming outfit on. Humor me. Erik's horrid at taking care of his injuries, and this would actually help him." The twinkle in Helene's eye made it clear she thought she was 'helping' us both.

Traitor.

"Saga?" Erik arched his brow. "What do *you* want to do?"

"I'd like to swim," I admitted. "But I'm not familiar with this beach. Are the tides safe?"

"At this time of day, we should be fine." Erik squinted at the ocean. "Just stick to the shoreline, and stay out of the way of the boats."

"Have a good time!" Helene jumped up, pulling me with her. "I'm going to see if Zaan needs any help. I've never reset a jaw before!"

With that, she skipped across the grass, her energy unnervingly joyful for a girl about to pop someone's face back into place.

"She has a seriously backwards idea of fun," I said.

"You don't know the half of it. Last year, she broke

my nose and tried to reset it herself." Erik tapped the slightly crooked bridge of his nose. "You see how that worked out."

"Ouch." I winced. "How'd that happen?"

"Believe it or not, I agreed to take her riding. The dragon bucked, she panicked, and . . ." Erik mimed jamming an elbow to my face.

"I take it you haven't brought her again?"

"No. Nor do I plan to. She's a danger to herself." Erik shook his head. "But her heart is pure goodness. When Helene's parents died, we worried she'd lose herself in grief. But she and Freia mourned together. Helene had two mothers, and though they weren't related to Freia by blood, they were absolutely her sisters-by-choice. Now my cousin is quite nearly her old self. God help us all."

Poor Helene. "What happened to her moms?"

"They were killed two years ago, defending our settlement on the mainland—Valkyris East." Erik shook his head. "Foreign raiders happened upon it, and though we were ultimately successful, our tribe wasn't without casualties."

Sorrow filled my heart. "I'm sorry to hear it."

"That's a part of life." Erik's eyes darkened. "But let's not dwell on it. Do you really want to swim, or were you saying that to get my cousin to leave you alone?"

"I do, actually. I swam every morning back home." It was warmer then, but when in Rome . . .

"I thought you lived on farmland?" Erik tilted his head.

Skit!

"Uh, in the lake," I blurted. "We had a really big lake. Nice for swimming."

Pants on fire.

"Fair enough. We'll head a safe distance from the rowers—try not to hurt yourself out there."

"I could say the same to you." I followed Erik across the lawn, around the wrestlers and sword fighters, and down to the little beach. He removed his pants and boots, leaving nothing more than a fitted pair of shorts to cover the impressive muscles of his butt. Heat rushed to my face, and I hurriedly pulled my dress over my head and stepped into the water.

The heat promptly disappeared.

"Holy God, this is cold!" I leapt back onto the shore.

"Hmm." Erik frowned.

"Why are you looking at me like that?" I rubbed my freshly goose-pimpled arms, and tried not to stare at Erik's naked chest. Or the thin piece of fabric that covered his man parts.

"I just didn't take you for delicate. That's all." Erik shrugged.

"I am not delicate!" I protested.

"Prove it." His eyes twinkled as he pointed to a log floating fifty yards offshore. "We swim to the log and back. Winner gets bragging rights, and their choice of afternoon activities."

My heart jackknifed. *Afternoon activities?* Was that his way of asking me on a date?

Play it cool, Saga. Don't let the hot Viking see you're into him.

I folded my arms across my chest. "It's on. Hope you like archery."

Erik's easy grin left me light-headed. "Hope *you* like *hnefatafl.*"

Whatever that was.

I stepped into the water, ignoring the insta-chatter of my teeth, and squared my shoulders to my target. "Call it."

"On three. Two. One. Go!"

Erik ran into the water, and I charged after him, ignoring the near-freezing temperature that buckled my knees and left me wishing I was *anywhere but here.* When he'd fully submerged himself and began his strokes, I held my breath, closed my eyes, and prepared to freeze my butt off.

Here goes nothing.

CHAPTER 21

THE WATER WAS EVEN colder than I'd feared. Icy waves doused my skin, stalling my breath and chilling my veins. I knew that movement would be my saving grace, but my limbs were frozen in place—as if motion of any kind might cause my frosty extremities to snap clean off. Nonetheless, I forced my legs up and down, pumping in a dolphin kick until my shoulders finally relaxed. I circled my arms and broke the surface, drawing a breath that filled my lungs with a slightly less intense chill. I lowered my head and swam, elongating my arm circles and maximizing my speed. The next time I drew a breath, I spotted Erik swimming nearby. He was close enough that I'd be able to catch up . . . if I didn't freeze to death first.

God bless the Norwegian ocean.

I kicked harder, increasing my speed and, hopefully, closing the gap between me and Erik. Since the saltwater stung my eyes I squeezed them shut, not opening them again until I lifted my head for another breath. In that interval, I spotted the log and adjusted my trajectory so I stayed on target. I returned my face to the water and pushed myself to up my pace. I did *not* want to lose. If Erik really had asked me on a date, I didn't want to end up spending it doing *hnef—kneff*—whatever he'd said.

Chess. The thing he said is that chess game Helene described. Right?

Gods, I *definitely* didn't want to spend our first date playing chess. Long walk in the rose garden, picnic by the sea, private rowboat around the island, all yes-es. But chess? Seriously?

My lungs begged for air, and I raised my head to draw a breath. I opened my eyes, zeroed in on the log, and realized I'd drawn even with Erik. If I could hold this pace around the turn and maintain it all the way back to shore, I would totally kick his butt!

Mmm, Erik's butt . . .

I put my head back in the water, and pushed myself even harder. By the time I reached the log, my arms screamed, my legs trembled, and the chill of the ocean had again seeped into my bones. I hadn't realized the turnaround was that far. I circled the log, raised my head to set the beach in my sights . . . and discovered I had swum *much* farther than I'd intended to. The shore was easily twice as far away as I'd expected it to be. A current must have swept the log out, which meant . . .

The realization crossed my mind a split second too late. Before I knew what was happening, a fierce wave dragged me beneath the water's surface. I clawed my way back up, where I had just enough time to draw a single gulp of air before I went under again. The ocean was *strong*. And from what I could gather, it was taking me *away* from where I wanted to go.

Oh, God.

It took all of my strength to kick my way to the surface again. This time, I was able to cry out before the water dragged me back below. "Help! There's a curr—"

Down I went, this time tumbling as a surge of water shifted my trajectory. It took everything I had not to panic. Losing control wouldn't do anything to get me to safety—though that was the most reasonable response to being hurtled *away* from my only source of air.

Another wave sent me tumbling and I forced my eyelids open, ignoring the sting from the saltwater as I struggled to discern which way was up. The sea to my right was the brightest, while my left seemed to be a tapestry of sand and rocks. Since the rocks were fairly close, and my energy was fairly low, I kicked *away* from the light, planted my feet firmly on the ocean floor, and used every ounce of strength to launch myself upward. When I broke the surface, I drew a long gulp of air, focused on treading water, and prayed another wave wouldn't take me under.

"Saga!" Erik's panicked shout came from too far away to be useful. "Don't fight the tide. I'm coming for you!"

"Okay!" I called weakly. I treaded in a circle until I spotted the blond head framed by thick arms cutting fiercely through the waves. Erik had nearly halved the distance between us when another wave pulled me down. This time I tumbled faster than before, spinning underwater in a dizzying circle until I collided with what felt like a slab of granite. A splitting pain ricocheted across my skull, sending excruciating jolts firing through my entire body. I was overwhelmed by an all-encompassing agony that stretched from my head to my toes. Air burst from my lips as I let out a silent scream, the rising bubble floating overhead as I surrendered to the pain. The last thing I remembered before my oxygen gave out was the shadow overhead. It was large, and powerful, and for reasons I couldn't quite piece together, its presence gave me the slightest degree of comfort.

And then my world fell utterly dark.

❄

"I need a healer!" The shout jarred me from unconsciousness, each word striking a sharp clap of fear through my body. Though anxiety crackled all around me, I felt only peace. My cheek was pressed against a warm surface that absolutely radiated protection. And though my body bobbed up and down, whoever was holding me moved with such surety that I couldn't feel anything but calm.

I was exactly where I needed to be.

I nestled closer to the warmth, turning so my nose was pressed against a smooth, taut surface. I drew a shaky breath, inhaling the scent of pine and saltwater before drifting into the darkness.

"She's bleeding." The words pulled me back out. They came with such urgency, such absolute terror, my stomach fluttered in sympathy. Someone was badly hurt. And this man, whoever he was, was worried sick.

Poor guy.

"Is she breathing?" A female voice spoke from nearby. Cool hands brushed against my face. I shivered away from the contact and they retracted. They returned seconds later, this time resting lightly atop my chest. "Good. I feel a heartbeat."

"She's breathing. But her head—it's losing a lot of blood." The man's voice wavered, and my heart tugged. He sounded familiar, but I couldn't quite place his voice—it was too distorted with worry.

"Gods," the female whispered. "Take her straight to the healing unit."

"There may not be time. Look at this." The man shifted me gently in his arms. "Can they work on her out here?"

"Oh, sweet girl." The cool hand stroked my cheek. "No. We don't want anything infecting that cut. Take her inside—I'll have a team meet you immediately."

"Thank you, Mother."

The cool hand disappeared, and I was once again bobbing lightly. My eyelids fluttered open, and through my haze I made out the blurry form of a massive man.

Beams of sunlight streamed around his face, giving him a near-angelic glow. Although worry furrowed his brow, and a hint of darkness tinged his normally sky-hued eyes, there was no mistaking the bearded jaw or unruly blond mane. It was Erik who carried me.

Which meant it was his chest my lips were touching.

Mmm.

"Hey," I mumbled lazily, my lips grazing hard muscles beneath soft skin. "Wharucaeeme?"

"Saga!" Erik's eyes met mine. Relief poured from their azure depths, filling me with a warmth that stretched from my heart all the way to my toes. But it disappeared as quickly as it had come as an icy chill wracked my body. Tremors rocked my extremities, and I pressed myself closer to Erik.

"I'm c-c-cold," I whispered. My teeth banged together, and I buried my face into Erik's chest. The movement sent a shock of pain across my head, leaving me wondering if an explosive had just detonated inside my skull. "Arugh!"

"Try not to move," Erik ordered. He must have picked up his pace, because the wind pressed harder against my back.

"Imperfkeewul," I whimpered. But as the not-quite-words came out, a wave of dizziness coursed through me. My head spun as if I were on an out of control merry-go-round, the forces so overwhelming that I tumbled slowly back into darkness.

The last thing I remembered were warm lips

pressed lightly against my forehead, murmuring the reassurance that everything would be okay.

He hoped.

❄

Light. Why was there so much light? Had I somehow found myself on the surface of the freaking sun?

I dragged my eyelids open, blinking fiercely against the barrage of beams beating down on my face. There were so many . . . tiny little daggers driving into my brain with the force of a thousand jackhammers. *Ouch.* I raised my arm to block out the light, but the movement sent agonizing jabs from my shoulder down my spine. Why was I so sore?

"You're awake." Erik's deep voice filled my ear. I shifted my eyes from the window to find him hovering anxiously at the foot of . . .

I was in a bed, but it wasn't mine. Where was I?

"Erik?" I tried to sit up, but motion proved impossible. Everything in my body ached.

"Stay still." Erik moved closer. He dropped to his knees before clasping warm fingers around mine. He was so tall—or this bed was so short, I couldn't tell— that when he knelt, our faces were level. "How are you feeling?"

"Sore." I winced. "Where am I? What happened?"

"You're in the healing unit. You've just had your head sewn back together."

What the actual hell?

My free hand flew to my scalp. I instantly regretted the movement.

"Ouch," I whimpered.

"Stay. Still." Erik gently wrapped long fingers around my wrist, and brought it back down. He clasped both of my hands in his as he spoke. "You struck your head in the ocean. You were underwater for a long time."

"I . . ." Fog addled my brain. I sifted through the haze of memories until I stumbled across a recent one. "We were racing."

"Yes." Clear, blue eyes bored into mine.

"And I was winning."

The eyes crinkled in the corners. "You can't prove that."

"I was," I declared. "And then . . . oh, God."

The events came rushing back. The strength of the wave. The terror of being sucked under. The fierce desire to live, even as I'd realized the ocean was an enemy I'd never overpower . . .

"Shh." Erik reached up, and the coarse pad of his thumb gently grazed my cheek. "Don't strain yourself."

"How did I . . ."

"I pulled you out."

"Thank you," I whispered.

Erik's thumb swiped again. I turned into the touch and he opened his hand, so my cheek nestled into his palm.

"It's my fault, Saga. I should have known the tides. But I've never seen one this strong—especially not at this time of day." Erik's shoulders hunched together, and for the first time, I noticed how pale he was. His face was drawn, exhausted. How long had he been at my side?

"I'm fine now," I mumbled.

Erik's thumb continued to trace my cheekbone. "I asked the *älva* keepers to make sure you stayed asleep while the healers worked on you. But you're likely to be in a substantial amount of pain once their magic wears off."

Crazy-hot Viking said what?

"Excuse me?"

"Sorry. I forget you're not from here." An unreadable emotion flickered across Erik's face. It disappeared before I could ask what it meant. "*Älva* are the fairies the gods gifted Valkyris when my parents established this island."

"I . . . kind of remember that."

"We try not to use their magic for personal gain— we reserve it for functions that benefit *all* of the tribe, like protecting the island or implementing castle-wide improvements. But you were nearing consciousness as the healers sewed your scalp, and I called in the keepers to put you back under." Erik's lips turned down. "The magic should dissipate soon, which means you're going to be in a lot of pain."

"But I'm here." I drew a slow breath. "You saved my life."

"It was my fault you were at risk in the first place. I should have kept us closer to the shore."

"You saved my life," I repeated. "Thank you."

Erik lowered his head so his forehead rested lightly against my arm. His tangled hair flowed messily across his shoulders, and I tentatively brought one hand up to touch it. It was soft against my fingertips, and a warmth filled my chest as I stroked the matted waves. Erik barely knew me and he'd risked his own life to save mine. Then he'd stayed with me through what sounded like one hell of a surgery . . . and called on magic fairies to make sure I didn't feel more pain than absolutely necessary. Either he actually liked me or . . .

No, that was it. Erik liked me.

Erik likes me?

My hand jolted at the realization, my fingers tangling in Erik's hair. He looked up, and I gently withdrew them.

"Are you hurting?" he asked.

"No," I whispered. "I'm just . . ."

Shocked.

"Saga." That incomprehensible look came over Erik's eyes again.

"Mmm?"

"You said something while you were under the *älva's* magic. You may have been dreaming, but . . ."

He looked so concerned; something must have been really wrong. "What is it?"

"Where are you from, Saga? Really?"

My stomach dropped. What had I said? "Um . . . I . . . well . . ."

"You're not from Norway."

"No," I whispered.

"And you're not from . . . now."

Oh, God. He knows.

"No." The word was barely more than a breath.

Understanding flickered across Erik's face. "Strange things have come from my mother using that dagger. I just didn't realize it could . . . it seems impossible."

"Erik, I . . ." I had absolutely no idea what to say.

Erik's thumb shifted to my jaw. "I'm sorry we took you from your world. This must be very overwhelming for you—all of it."

He finds out you're from the future and his first reaction is . . . sympathy? Who the hell is this guy?

Moisture pooled in my eyes. "It's been a rough month and a half."

"I'll bet." Erik gently wiped my tear away. "Is it very different, where you're from?"

"Completely." I grimaced. "Nobody kidnaps you, or forces you into marriage, or sells you as a slave. We don't have any dragons, or fairies, or raids, or . . . well, any of this."

"What do you have?"

"Coffee, for one," I muttered, before raising my voice. "And more things like your flameless candles and hot baths. Things are different—easier, in a lot of ways. But harder in others. Where I'm from, tight-knit communities like Valkyris are rare. And my people aren't nearly as self-reliant as yours. Vikings are extremely productive. Surely, you know this."

"Vikings?"

"It's what we call your people in my time. Raiders, explorers, Norse warriors . . . Vikings."

"Interesting." Erik studied the ceiling. "But I don't understand how, Saga. *How* did that dagger bring you from then . . . to now? And when is then?"

"Then—my then—is a little more than a thousand years ahead of your now. I think."

A low whistle escaped Erik's lips. "My gods."

"You're telling me."

"And . . . *how*?"

"I honestly don't know. One minute, I was swimming in the sea. And the next, I'd touched the dagger and . . ." I raised my shoulder, the movement pulling uncomfortably on ocean-battered muscles. "Ouch."

"Try not to move," Erik reminded me.

I gave an infinitesimal nod. "I ended up in the same place, but where there had been enormous trees and redwood-decked houses, there were log cabins and a considerably shorter forest. And a group of ships had just arrived to raid the village. Clan Bjorn mistook me for the invading party's heir, and . . . well, you know the rest."

"My gods." Erik rested his forehead on mine. "I'm so sorry."

"It's not your fault." I closed my eyes. He was so close, if I lifted my chin just two inches our lips would be touching. And since I was already lying down, it wouldn't take much effort to pull Erik on top of me and . . .

No, Saga. You just had your scalp sewn back together. No ravaging the Viking.

Not until your head stops bleeding.

At the thought, a searing pain shot from the back of my skull to my temples. It ricocheted across my forehead, overwhelming me with intensity. "Owwwww," I moaned.

"I've hurt you." Erik pulled away, regret lining his perfect features.

"No. I think the magic wore—arugh!"

"Healers!" Erik bellowed. "Get in here!"

Through my pain-fog, I barely made out two white-clad women racing through the door.

"What's happened?" one asked.

"What can you give Saga for her pain?" Erik demanded.

Sympathy lined the women's faces. "We can't infuse her with any more magic—her system won't be able to process it. The best we can offer is an herb."

"Then give her the *jævla* herb!" Erik swore.

"Right away." One of the women rushed from the room, while the other hastened to my side. I moaned as she adjusted the pillow beneath my head.

"We need to keep you elevated," she apologized.

"'Kay," I whimpered.

Erik stepped back as the second healer returned with a tiny ball of leaves and a cup of water. "Chew this, and swallow it down," she said softly. "It won't completely eliminate the pain, but it will soften it."

I tried to reach for the cup, but my muscles screamed in protest. "Ow!"

"Here." Erik took the items from the healer. He held the herb to my mouth. I parted my lips, shivering at the feel of his fingers against them. When I'd chewed whatever passed for medicine in these parts, Erik raised the cup and helped me drink. He wiped a droplet from my bottom lip, sending another shiver coursing through me. In spite of my pain, I was suddenly very, very warm.

"How long will it take?" Erik asked.

"Just a few minutes," the first healer said. "Until then, the best thing she can do is rest."

"I'll wait with her." Erik dropped to his knees again, clasping one of my hands in both of his.

"She's going to be here for a few days," cautioned the second healer. "And this herb is going to make her sleep—it's the best way to get her through the worst of her pain."

Please, please God, gods, and whoever else is listening. Let me sleep through this mind-numbing agony. Kisses, Saga.

"I'll find a chair once she's asleep, then," Erik said.

"We'll have one sent in for you along with some food—you've both been here for hours. Are you hungry yet, Miss Saga?" The first healer paused at the foot of my bed.

"No," I whimpered. "I just want to stop hurting."

"I know you do," she said sympathetically. "Close

your eyes, and let the herb do its job. If you need anything, Erik will fetch us."

"Thanks," I mumbled. The room swam in and out of focus, whether from the herb or my body's inability to tolerate this level of pain, I did not know. But as the healers carried in a chair, then left, and as Erik settled determinedly at my side, I allowed myself to float back into the darkness. The last things I remembered before I passed out were the intoxicating cocktail of pine and saltwater, warm lips pressing against my forehead, and the soft murmur of a voice that brought me more comfort than I had any right to expect, wishing me pleasant dreams.

"I'll be here when you wake up," Erik vowed.

And I had no doubt that he would be.

CHAPTER 22

I SPENT A FULL week and a half in the healing unit. And Erik came to visit me every single day.

Helene came too. Usually she smuggled in chocolate, which we threw down while she filled me in on the latest academy gossip. But on my third day, she arrived with a fresh batch of lefse that she'd cooked in her homemaking class. Thankfully, she also brought some lefse from the castle kitchen, which we ate when we discovered Helene's had the consistency of soggy bricks.

Bless her heart.

Axel remained absent, but I knew he was still on his mission with Clan Bjorn. I hoped he'd been able to reach Ingrid and Vidia, and I hoped even more that they were well on their way to helping the assassin . . . and earning their freedom.

Katrin visited often. The first time, she brought the most current transcription list for the coffee and fork shipment we'd been working on, along with a plea that I get better soon so she didn't have to be alone with Brigga anymore. I'd laughed so hard at that, the healers had to give me another dose of the herb so I didn't pull any stitches. One day, Helene and Katrin had shown up at the same time, and our giggles were so loud, the healers threatened to kick my friends out. The two girls had been close long before I'd come to Valkyris, their bond solidified by a shared love of learning, and a shared dislike of Brigga and Birna, who apparently tortured *all* the smart girls.

They *so* had it coming.

On my fourth afternoon in the healing unit, Katrin and Helene decided to teach me Viking chess.

"*Hnefatafl*," Katrin corrected the third time I called it by its American name. "Chest makes no sense."

"*Chess*," I said. "In my tribe we call it *chess*."

"That makes even less sense." Helene shook her head. "That's not even a real word."

I gave up after that.

Freia and Halvar visited too. Ever the mother hen, Freia fussed over me for the better part of an hour, making sure I had soft pillows, warm blankets, and all the food I could eat. She'd come on Waffle Day, proudly bearing a fresh batch from the kitchen, which we enjoyed with afternoon tea. The three of us sat around the little table in my room, enjoying waffles with fresh lingonberry jam, and a fruity tea that tasted nothing like the horrible blend I'd had my first morning with Erik. Though I was dying to ask about the war talk I'd overheard in the church, the two chiefs kept the conversation light, flitting from discussion about a new long ship the academy students had built, to which of my classmates had done well in that weekend's sporting events, to the rumor of a new shipment from one of the northernmost tribes that contained a whole new style of paint. I knew the chiefs had much on their minds, and I appreciated them taking time to check in on me.

But Erik's visits were my favorite.

By the end of my stay, I was allowed to walk the halls, and sit up for two hours at a time. I'd had too long to stew on thoughts of war, and prophesies, and angry, brooding men named Raynor—whoever he was. So, when Erik arrived for his evening visit, I was sitting at my little table, Viking chess laid out for play. I'd distract him with competition while I drew nuggets of information from his vault-like brain. I doubted he'd volunteer any information about what I'd overheard that night in the church, but maybe if I talked around the subject I could get him to share just enough to put my mind at ease. And in the process, I could learn more about his life as Valkyris' heir, and the larger world that had shaped him.

Maybe I was meant to be a strategist, after all.

"*Hei*." Erik smiled as he walked into my room. He placed a still-steaming batch of lefse on the table, and dropped into the chair across from mine. "You're sitting up. You must be feeling well."

"Well enough to kick your butt." I grinned.

Erik arched one blond brow.

"You ready to lose to a girl?" I tilted my head toward the chessboard.

"I've lost to girls plenty of times. My cousin is vicious at *hnefatafl*." A sly grin stretched across Erik's face. "But I have no intention of losing to you. Newcomer."

The flame of competition sparked in my chest. "Oh, it's on. Viking."

Erik leaned forward on his elbows. "What are the stakes?"

"Winner picks what we do tomorrow. Hey, don't you still owe me from our last bet? Before the ocean attacked me, I was *clearly* beating you at swimming."

Erik chuckled. "Fair enough. Your move."

I picked up the tiny wooden chess piece, and positioned it in what Katrin had taught me was the strongest opening move. Erik countered, and in no time we were immersed in a thoroughly competitive game.

Stage one, complete. Now to pull out the information.

"So." I picked up a piece of lefse and took a bite. "Jeez, this is good."

"Agreed." Erik captured one of my men before taking a bite of his own. "Axel prefers the waffles, but his tastes are less refined."

Snort.

"How's it going with Axel?" I asked as I scooped up

one of Erik's pieces. "It's been a while since he left—any word?"

"None." Erik frowned as he studied the board. "He took one of the dragons, so the trip there shouldn't have taken more than a few days. He must have decided to stay nearby—oversee the mission from the ground. If that's the case, he could be gone several weeks—maybe even months."

"It's already been a month." I blinked. "He hasn't let you know how it's going yet?"

"He hasn't." Erik captured another piece and dropped it into his pile.

"Should he have?"

"He'll usually touch base if a mission's going to take more than a week or two," Erik admitted.

"Erik. That's not good." I lowered my hands, our game forgotten.

"Like I said, he's probably overseeing on-site. If he felt your friends were at risk, he wouldn't have wanted to leave them."

"Or Lars could have captured him, and figured out he's with us. Showing up on a dragon would have been a dead giveaway. We're the only tribe who has them, right?"

"Correct." Erik frowned. "But Axel's a seasoned warrior. The odds of him being captured are extremely slim."

"Are you sure?" I pushed at my cuticles.

"I'm sure." Erik reached across the table. He took

one of my hands in his, sending a warm pulse up my arm. *Yum.*

"Okay," I whispered.

Erik squeezed my fingertips. "Odds are, he found one—or both—of your friends attractive, and has been amusing himself before bringing them home."

I rolled my eyes. "I love Axel, but Ingrid and Vidia are way too smart to go for a player."

"A what?" Erik asked.

"Never mind." I shook my head. "So, we're not worried?"

"Not yet. If he hasn't returned in a few more weeks, I'll send a rider out to check on him."

"Good." I nodded, withdrawing my hand and capturing two of Erik's men in one move. "Also, checkmate."

"Hmm?"

"It's what we say in my time at this point in the game. You're done for."

Erik chuckled. "Who taught you to play *hnefatafl*?"

"Helene and Katrin. Why?"

"They taught you wrong. *This* is a checkmate." Erik jumped two of my men, moving his piece into a winning position.

Well, skit.

"Two out of three?" I asked hopefully.

"Are you really prepared to lose to me twice?"

"In your dreams." I quickly reset the pieces and made the first move. "You're going down."

"If you say so." Erik captured one of my men with an easy smile.

"So . . ." I waited for Erik to make his next move. "Is everything else going okay, inter-tribe wise?"

"What do you mean?"

"I don't know." I took my turn, and waited again. "No skirmishes? Disputes? Impending world-ending wars I should be preparing for?"

I'd tried to keep my tone relaxed, but Erik froze with his fingers on a chess piece. "What did Helene tell you?"

"Helene? Nothing. Why? What does Helene know?"

"Helene doesn't know anything. But her prophet friends are horrid gossips." Erik knocked one of my pieces aside before withdrawing his hand.

"I actually overheard *you*," I said casually. "I was, uh, out for a walk that night you were in the church and I couldn't help but hear the shouting."

"Raynor." Erik shook his head. "What did you hear?"

I leaned forward on my elbows. "Are we going to war? Be honest with me."

"All right. Honestly? I don't know." Erik ran a hand through his wild mane. "Our prophets have foreseen a battle that leads to the end of one of the tribes. But whether that tribe is ours, another, or one completely removed from our circle of influence, they've not yet determined."

"Would we be involved in a battle that big?"

"We generally stay out of matters that aren't our concern," Erik said. "But the prophets wouldn't have brought this to my parents' attention if they didn't believe it would affect us."

I wrung my hands together. "Do you think it has anything to do with Axel's mission? Is Clan Bjorn going to attack us because . . ." *Because I asked you to help my friends?*

God, if I'd risked the entire future of Erik's tribe . . .

Erik reached across the table. He used his thumb to gently tug my bottom lip from between my teeth. "If Clan Bjorn has any reason to attack, it is owing to a long series of disputes between our tribes. You, *min kjære*, are the least of their concerns."

"You stole me from them," I reminded him. "Lars was livid."

"Lars doesn't like being shown up. Especially not in front of a beautiful girl."

Heat flooded my neck. "But—"

"But nothing. If Valkyris is to go to war, Freia and Halvar will weigh the risks against the gains, consult their war council, and pray over what is for the greatest good of the greatest number. The burden won't be on your shoulders."

"I guess." I studied my lap.

"Saga." Erik lifted my chin with two fingers. "None of this is your fault. Clan Bjorn is a barbaric tribe, as are many of the allies. One day, Valkyris will be charged with righting their wrongs. That has nothing to do with you."

"Okay." I offered Erik a tentative smile. He stroked my chin with the softest imaginable touch.

Mmm.

"Now, are you going to worry all day or can I get back to . . . how did you put it? Kicking your butt at *hnefatafl*?"

I snorted, my laughter so loud I attracted the attention of a white-clad woman. She stepped into my room with a frown.

"What did we tell you about your stitches?" the healer admonished.

"Sorry," I chortled. "Erik made me do it."

She clucked her tongue before retreating to the hallway.

I swatted Erik's arm. "You're going to get me in trouble."

"You need a bit of trouble in your life." Erik's eyes moved slowly from my chin to my cleavage, appreciation reflected in their clear, blue depths. My heart quickened, thumping against my ribcage so fiercely that I was certain he could see it. By the time his eyes moved back to my face, a ravenous hunger sparked from their now smoky depths. His chest rose heavily as he drew a slow breath, and the muscles of his forearms flexed as he gripped the edge of the table.

"You'd better make your move," he growled.

My God. Did he mean . . .?

Erik tapped the chess board with one finger.

Oh. Right. Chess.

Stupid chess.

"Okay," I whispered. I forced my eyes from his, and shakily shifted one of my pieces.

We didn't speak for the rest of the game, and by the time he finally left my room, my body was buzzing with pent-up tension. He hadn't touched me again—not so much as a hand squeeze, or a playful shoulder push when he'd beaten me for the second time. But I'd wanted him to. God only knew how much I'd wanted him to do that . . . and so much more.

That Viking was going to be the death of me.

CHAPTER 23

THE DAY BEFORE I was discharged, I was permitted an hour-long field trip. The healers said it was a test—if I could successfully maneuver around Valkyris without incurring additional injury, they would release me in the morning. But if I complained of any dizziness, discomfort, or otherwise seemed unwell on my return, I'd be facing another week in the healing unit.

Obviously, I was going to Viking up and return with a smile. No way was I living through another week of bed rest.

Without coffee.

Helene had volunteered to walk with me, but the healers thought Erik would be a more suitable chaperone. Something about muscles for days, and the ability to carry me in one arm while slaying dragons with the other. At least, that was my interpretation of "he's superior in strength and dexterity, Saga."

The outside temperatures had dropped considerably during my stay. Fall was nearly over, and the seamstresses had sent over two new, long-sleeved dresses—one cream with blue stitching, the other red with white embroidery. Each dress had a contrasting under-layer which popped against the primary color, and a complementary shawl. Step one of my discharge test was dressing myself, and after considerable thought I decided to wear the cream and blue dress. Although my bruises had faded, my muscles still ached, which meant dressing took longer than I had any intention of admitting. But I did it.

Baby steps.

My palms smoothed the front of the thick wool fabric, and I wondered if the seamstresses meant for it to so perfectly match Erik's eyes. As I fastened the silver clasps that framed the square neckline, a light rapping echoed from my door. I hurriedly adjusted the blue shawl around my shoulders, checked my long, loose hair for flyaways, and drew a steadying breath.

Here we go.

"Come in."

The door opened, revealing the wide shoulders and unruly mane of my chaperone. Erik had dressed for the chill—his long-sleeved tunic was covered with an elbow-length cloak, and a stretch of fabric wrapped over his pants, from ankle to knee. And he'd weaponed up—a long sword hung from his belt, and a dagger was tucked into the pouch at his waist.

Wait. Dagger?

My heart quickened as I studied the gem-less handle of the blade. Disappointment surged through me as I realized this wasn't *my* dagger—it was just a standard weapon.

But God, did Erik look good wearing it.

"Rough day?" I nodded at the pair of blades.

"You could say that." Erik rested his hand against his sword's hilt. "I believe you were promised leave?"

"One hour." I grinned. "One *glorious* hour of fresh air and sunshine and—"

"And snow."

Wait. What?

"Already?" I moved to the window and peeked through the glass. Sure enough, a light dusting of white covered the ground outside the castle. It stretched across the gardens, coating the lavender and roses in a thin layer of frost. "Isn't it early?"

"It usually doesn't come for another week or two, but we have fairly long winters in the north. Is that different in your time?"

"I'm not sure. Maybe." Climate change was a definite issue, but I'd never spent a fall in Norway—I'd always gone back to Minnesota at the start of the school year. And with the lack of calendars at the academy, I wasn't entirely sure what day it was, anyway. Maybe late October/early November snowfalls were the norm.

"Will you be warm enough?" Erik asked.

"Probably. And we'll only be out for an hour, so . . ."

Erik offered his arm. "Walk with me?"

"God, yes. Get me out of this place." I wrapped my fingers around his forearm, ducking my head at the pulse that shot straight to my heart. It thumped against my ribcage as Erik led me down the corridor and out of the healing unit. He pushed the wooden outer door, opening it to reveal a brilliantly lit wonderland. The clouds were thin enough that beams of sunlight streamed across Valkyris. They bounced off the ocean, illuminating the castle and sparkling against the tapestry of white. And the air . . .

I inhaled slowly, the crisp breeze chilling my lungs. It smelled of new beginnings—the changing of seasons, the shifting of tides . . . *tides.*

At my shudder, Erik glanced down in concern. "You're cold," he deduced.

"No. Just thinking about the last time I was outside."

Erik's lips tugged downward. "Would you like to go back to the castle?"

"Absolutely not. I was promised a walk, and I'm not setting foot in that building for another fifty-eight minutes."

Erik covered my hand with his. "Think you can make it as far as the rose garden?"

"You seriously underestimate me. You do know that, right?"

Amusement danced across Erik's face. He tugged me gently forward, our feet crunching in the thin layer of snow. "You look lovely today, Saga. I'm not used to seeing your hair out of braids."

"This is how I wore it back home," I said quietly.

Erik's eyes shifted from sky-blue to midnight as he studied the waves that tumbled halfway down my back. "It suits you."

Heat climbed up my neck, the chill long forgotten.

We walked in silence until we reached the garden. I held tight to Erik's forearm, not only to avoid wobbling and thereby show the healers I was *totally* capable of being released, but also because, well . . . *Erik's forearm.* He kept his other hand on mine, gently stroking the backs of my fingers as we walked. It took everything I had not to dissolve into a pool of hormones at the touch.

Viking up, Saga. Remember?

Right.

We'd just reached the inside of the rose garden when Erik shot me a curious look.

"What?"

"I have so many questions," he admitted. "But I haven't wanted to overwhelm you when you're meant to be focused on your healing."

"Please. I am more tired of healing than you could possibly imagine."

Erik tilted his head so his hair fell over his shoulder. I resisted the ridiculous urge to reach up and touch it. "You're sure?"

"Overwhelm me," I demanded.

"All right." Erik led us through the frost-covered blooms. "Do you miss it? Your home?"

"Terribly," I said. "I was meant to start college—uh. An upper-level school. I was going to study international relations, and apply for a summer internship with the United Nations. Everything was all laid out. And then . . ."

"And then my mother magicked you here."

I paused to study a snow-covered rose. Pale pink petals peeked from beneath a light layer of ice. "My grandma always said I was too uptight—that I needed to learn how to roll with life's changes. But I've always liked knowing how things were going to play out. There's enough unpredictability, so I choose to control what I can." I sniffed the bloom. Its fragrance was barely discernable through the frost. "Look where that got me."

"This must be overwhelming." Erik rubbed the back of my hand. "I can't imagine the worry it's caused you."

"Mostly I'm worried for my family. Mormor must be beside herself—she already lost her daughter and son-in-law—my mom and dad. I can't imagine what she's feeling now that her granddaughter's gone too."

"I'm sorry you lost your parents," Erik said soberly.

"It was years ago." I smiled sadly. "But thank you."

Erik nodded.

"I just wish I could let my family know that I'm okay. But even if I knew where the dagger was, I don't think I could get it to activate again. I tried back at the *Ting*, but I couldn't figure out how to make it work."

Erik paused. "Do you want to go home?" Blue eyes pierced mine, the unspoken question hovering between us.

Do you want to leave Valkyris?

"Is there a reason for me to stay?" I croaked.

The words hung in the air for an endless beat. Neither of us moved.

Erik's lips parted and he drew a breath, as if he were about to speak. But after a moment, he closed his mouth and lowered his gaze to his boots.

Oh . . .

My heart dropped, icy as the snow-covered ground.

"My life is there," I reminded him . . . and myself. "My home is there. And this world is . . ."

"I understand." Erik's voice was so soft, I had to strain to hear him. "You didn't ask for any of this."

"Neither did you." I was determined to keep a brave face. Never mind that he'd just crushed my heart. "Being Valkyris' heir must be . . . a lot of pressure."

"It is." Erik's jaw tensed. "I have fewer freedoms than Axel. But I have more privileges as well. It's . . . complicated."

"How so?" I asked softly.

"Well, for starters, I was never meant to lead. That was to be my sister's job."

"You have a sister?" I'd just assumed Erik was an only child.

"I had a sister," he said softly.

Oh. *Oh.*

Sadness washed over me, and I reached up to rest my fingertips over Erik's heart. "Oh, Erik."

"Liana was the perfect heir. Dutiful, smart, and not a selfish bone in her body. My parents raised her to put the needs of her people before herself, which would have been her greatest strength as a leader. But it ended up being the weakness that led to her—"

Erik's voice cracked, and he pressed his lips firmly together. His heartache was so palpable, I wanted to throw my arms around him and tell him everything would be okay. If I'd thought it would help, I would have done just that. Instead, I kept my palm pressed to his chest and said simply, "I'm so sorry."

"She died in the same battle that claimed Helene's mothers. They'd escorted her to our mainland colony, where she taught a monthly lesson to the school-children. The foreign raiders arrived before she could evacuate, and my aunts tried to protect her but—" Erik finally looked up, infinite pain pooling in his eyes.

Katrin's comment about Erik losing someone he loved finally made sense.

"You think you could have saved her," I remembered.

"I know I could have. If I'd been there, I would have murdered the monsters before I let them lay a finger on my sister."

"But your aunts were warriors," I reminded him. "And probably had much more battle experience than you did. There's nothing more you could have done."

"My brain knows that's true. But I can't stop thinking if only I'd been there . . ."

"Don't," I said firmly. "What-ifs will drive you crazy."

Erik drew a breath. "That's the reason I push you so

hard. You need to be able to protect yourself if we're ever attacked, and I'm not around to look out for you."

"Aw, Erik. You do care." I winked, earning my first smile in a full five minutes.

Score, Saga.

"It's my fault you're here. My parents hadn't prepared me like they had Liana—I was always meant to be the spare. And I was nowhere near the leader she'd been groomed to be. After she died, my mother threw herself into training me—trying to get me to absorb in two years everything my sister had spent two decades learning. I was . . . reluctant. And my mother grew desperate."

"She told me she used the dagger to track down a leader," I admitted. "She thinks I'm meant to help your tribe in some way."

"You already have." Erik covered my hand with his, pressing it to his heart. "You've reminded me what we fight for—and of what we stand to lose. And I've realized my parents are right . . . I can't do this job alone."

Alone? Does he mean . . .

"Helene told me you were supposed to get married last year," I blurted.

"Helene talks too much," Erik muttered.

"She said you were under a lot of pressure. Is that still . . . a thing?" Lord. This was *so* none of my business. But I'd started down this path, and I couldn't stop myself.

"With the threat of war, Freia wants to see the future of Valkyris secured. I understand, but . . ."

"You don't want to be forced into something you're not ready for."

"That." Erik's eyes met mine. "And I was waiting for the right girl."

Heat rippled across my skin. God, when he looked at me like that, the rest of the world just . . . fell away.

If only it were that easy.

Erik raised his hand to my head. He lightly threaded his fingers through my hair and cradled my cheek in his palm. "You're different than I thought you'd be, Saga. When I was sent to retrieve the dagger—to bring home a leader for our people—I knew whoever it brought me to would be strong, and capable, and intelligent. Valkyris demands nothing less. But I didn't expect your warmth—your independence. The way you fought off Lars, and refused to yield to me . . . that earned you my respect. But knowing what you've lost —and never once complained . . . that's earned my admiration."

My breath caught in my throat. "Erik, look—"

"It needs to be said," he interrupted. "Nothing about this is uncomplicated, but the gods brought you here, and—"

"No. *Look*." I pointed above me, where an enormous shadow darkened the sky. It passed through the clouds, rocketing to the ground with the speed of a runaway train. It pulled up seconds before it struck the earth, shifting out of alignment with the sun to reveal enormous green wings that stretched from a scaly, leathery torso. The dragon touched down just outside of the rose garden, tilting its head back and emitting a massive ball of fire into the air. I stepped closer to Erik as the dragon's rider slid off its back. With his tall, lanky frame, and piercing blue eyes, he was easily recognizable as the angry dissenter from the church confrontation. He marched toward us with a confident gait, and as I studied his square jaw and perfect cheekbones, I understood why he'd been with the Halvarssons . . . and why Freia had been so concerned by his outburst.

As the newcomer stalked through the garden gates, his gaze fell on me. One corner of his mouth turned up in a sneer, and the look in his eyes let me know he was none-too-impressed by my proximity to the Valkyris heir. But the look he gave Erik . . . *yikes.* If looks could kill, Erik would have been dead and set to sea, Viking-funeral style. Clearly, there was no love lost between these two. And as much as I wanted to believe their bad blood was a new development, my gut told me things went back farther.

About eighteen years farther.

Erik wrapped his arm around my waist, and pulled me close to his side. My theory was confirmed when he brought his head to mine, and whispered softly in my ear.

"Holy *skit.*" Erik swore. "My brother's home at last."

CHAPTER 24

THERE WAS A BROTHER? And said brother was the bat-*skit* crazy guy who'd just shown up on a dragon?

Can my life get any more insane?

"Stay behind me," Erik murmured. "And no matter what happens, do not go anywhere with him."

Like I was going to.

"Raynor." Erik kept his voice steady, but his hand trembled slightly at my waist. *Oh, boy.* "Where have you been?"

"Recruiting," Raynor replied. He walked steadily toward us, his boots crunching lightly on the snow. "In case you hadn't noticed, our numbers are nowhere near strong enough to go to war. And since you and Mother refuse to engage thralls—"

"And where are your recruits?" Erik's chest rumbled. "If you've compromised our location, so help me, Odin, I'll—"

"Relax. They're being vetted by Valkyris East. If they pass the inquiries, the mainland will send word."

Erik's eyes narrowed as he stared his brother down. They were similar in height, each at least six and a half feet tall, but while Erik was a broad-shouldered bulk of pure muscle, his brother was leaner, hungrier. My gut told me his strength was in his cunning . . . and possibly his willingness to betray the ones he was sworn to defend.

Raynor was bad news. Of this, I was one hundred percent certain.

As if sensing my distaste, Raynor's eyes shifted to me. His lip curled up again, and he spoke my name like it was a bad word. "Saga."

Erik shifted his body so he stood slightly in front of me.

"You must be the keeper Mother brought in to make sure my brother does his job."

"That's enough," Erik growled. "If you have nothing more to report, take your dragon and get out of here."

Raynor cocked his head at me. "Aren't you supposed to encourage Erik to collect *all* the information before dismissing a source?"

What the hell was he talking about?

"If you have something to say, say it," I said evenly. "Otherwise, I'd suggest you do as Erik says."

A spark illuminated Raynor's eyes. "I like her, Brother." His lips quirked as he noticed Erik's hand on my waist. "And, I'm gathering, so do you."

Erik's hand tightened around his sword. "If you have information pertinent to the safety of Valkyris—"

"All right, all right." Raynor waved his hand. "No need to draw your weapon. I just wanted you to know that two of the tribes have been engaged in secret meetings. Representatives of Bjorn and Jotir returned to the *Ting* shortly after it concluded, and have been in some kind of negotiation ever since."

"What are their terms?" Erik asked.

"I don't know. That information came from one of the recruits—a Clan Aestra thrall. He was retrieving forgotten items from one of the campsites when he overheard two Ragnar warriors talking. The meetings are so secretive, both parties brought a team of guards to discourage eavesdroppers."

My hand slid up Erik's bicep and held tight. This wasn't good.

"Are any other tribes involved in the meetings?" Erik asked.

"Again, I don't know. My recruit was lucky to escape unnoticed. But if two of the allies have gathered, the rest are likely to follow. They're planning to move against someone. The only question remaining is . . . is it us?"

My throat caught. As uneasy as Raynor made me, I knew he was right—unless that mainland settlement was massive, Valkyris didn't have the numbers to take on the rest of the allied tribes. Hell, we'd be lucky to win against just two tribes. I'd seen how those Bjorn warriors had handled intruders on their beach. They hadn't left a single raider alive.

Gulp.

"We need more warriors," I whispered.

A cold grin stretched across Raynor's face. "Now I *really* like her."

I looked up at Erik. "How many do we have on the mainland?"

"Not enough." Erik turned to his brother. "How many recruits have you brought in?"

"Fifty," Raynor said. "Most were thralls, left behind to clean up after the *Ting.* I offered them a silver coin apiece, and they trotted after me like sheep. They're not big on loyalty, slaves."

I bit the inside of my cheek to keep from shouting. "You clearly don't know much about them."

Raynor sneered. "Then enlighten me, *keeper.*"

A low growl built in Erik's chest, and I squeezed his bicep. "He's not worth it."

Nobody who couldn't see beyond a title was.

"Go out and collect as many new recruits as you can," Erik commanded. "Send them to Valkyris East, and see that our warriors there commence their training immediately."

"And what will you do? Amuse yourself with your new prize?" Raynor's gaze swept up and down my body. My stomach clenched, and I stepped closer to Erik.

"Look at her like that one more time, and you'll find yourself on the wrong end of a broadsword," Erik growled. "You're a single misstep away from losing your standing in my tribe. Watch yourself, *Brother*."

Raynor's eyes clouded with hatred. He spun on his heel and stormed back to his dragon, climbing atop its back and launching into the sky before I'd managed a proper exhale.

And I thought my *life was complicated.*

The bicep beneath my palm began to tremble, and when I looked up, white puffs emerged from between Erik's lips. His breath came in short bursts, the warm air turning to smoke in the chill. And his eyes . . .

I'd never seen a look quite like it. Pain mixed with distaste mixed with . . . was it anger? Sorrow? Fear?

Whatever it was, it passed in an instant. Erik schooled his face in an impassive mask, released his grip on his sword, and turned his body to mine.

"Saga." The word was thick with regret.

"Yes?"

"I'll help you get home. You're right; your life is there. Your family is there. And nothing good awaits you here."

You do. You're here.

I wanted to shout the words—bludgeon him over the head with them, if need be. Yes, I wanted to go home. Well, I was pretty sure I did. War and crazy brothers and dragons were here. But . . .

Doesn't he want me to stay?

I scanned Erik's face, barely recognizing the man in front of me. The friend who'd visited me in the healing unit was gone, replaced by a stoic, impassive warrior. "Erik?"

"War *is* coming, Saga. It's unavoidable. Whether it's now, or two years from now, our beliefs threaten the way things have always been done. We *will* be attacked, and we *will* rise to defend our way of life. There's no reason for you to be caught in the middle of all of that."

"I thought I was supposed to help you," I said quietly. "To protect this amazing world your family has created—to help your tribe offer hope to those who need it most."

Erik's face softened. "You have helped me. You've shown me there are good people out there who are worth fighting for. And who will fight alongside us because it's the right thing to do. For everyone."

My throat tightened.

"I know where my mother keeps her dagger, and I know where she takes it to pray. I'm fairly certain I'll be able to activate it there. We'll get you home, one way or another. Tomorrow."

Tomorrow.

It was so soon. *Too soon.* But it was the right thing to do. It was what Erik wanted. It was what *I* wanted.

Wasn't it?

CHAPTER 25

ERIK KNOCKED ON MY door early the next morning. The healers signed off on my discharge, and I followed him numbly down the long hallway out of the castle, and into the post-dawn chill. I'd told the healers I'd be back later to pick up my things, knowing full well I'd never see them again. This —all of this—was about to become a memory. Something that faded into the recesses of my mind, until I no doubt wondered if I'd dreamed the entire experience.

Maybe I have.

A light wind cut across the island, and I pulled my cloak tight around my body. I'd chosen the red dress today—the one with the white embroidery down the center. It popped against the grey mist rising off the ocean, a surge of color on the temporarily bleak landscape. I knew in a few hours the fog would burn off, and Valkyris would once again be a sea of green and blue and white. But in this moment, there was only grey.

The island matched my mood.

Erik marched silently beside me, his own cloak fluttering in the breeze. We hadn't spoken since he'd picked me up, and the silence between us was deafening. In the short time I'd known him, I'd never seen him so tense—not when he'd challenged a vengeful Lars, or when he'd squared off against his own brother. As we made our way across the snow-dusted heather, Erik's fists were balled, his jaw locked, and his eyes bore the steely determination of a predator about to strike. Something must have happened overnight—a new development with the war maybe, or another issue with his brother. The dark circles beneath his sky-blue eyes made me wonder if Erik had slept at all.

A horn sounded, and Erik picked up his pace. I lifted my skirt and hurried to match his steps. I knew that call—the castle would be awake soon; the entire island was about to become a hub of activity. Every hour of daylight was precious here, and all of Valkyris would be tending to crops, training to fight, and disseminating the information acquired by a nation of explorers. I'd miss their work ethic; their thirst for knowledge; their willingness to put the needs of the weak above their own enviable lifestyle. But most of all, I'd miss . . .

I'm going to miss him.

I studied the broad-chested Viking whose long

strides had carried him several paces ahead of me. Loose waves of hair tumbled around his shoulders, and his white-knuckled fist clung tightly to the hilt of his mother's dagger. My dagger. The one that was about to carry me a thousand years forward in time, away from this place, away from what might well have been a true connection . . . if it weren't for wars, and dragons, and brothers, and the millennium that separated our births. In another lifetime, maybe Erik and I would have made a good match. I'd never know.

God, this sucked.

Erik came to a stop, his snow-dusted boots planting squarely in the center of a low hill. We were on the far side of the island—behind the Dragehus, and well out of view of the castle. With the island still awakening, the only sound was the gentle lapping of the waves against the shore . . . and the words that sent my stomach plummeting to my feet.

"We're here."

Erik's voice was no more than a whisper. When he turned to face me, there was pain—honest-to-God pain —etched across his otherwise perfect face. He brought one hand to his cheek, stroking the blond fibers of his neatly trimmed beard as he massaged his jaw. "Guess we'd better get started."

"Erik, wait." I folded my hands together, and squeezed my eyes shut. *Brave. I am brave.* "I just want you to know that . . . I really appreciate what you did for me. If you hadn't saved me from Lars, I don't want to think about how horrible my life here would have been. You welcomed me into your home, and made sure I knew how to protect myself—though I still think a bow and arrow are far superior to some clunky sword, and . . . I . . ." *Spit it out, already.* "And I just want you to know that you mean a lot to me. I'll never forget you."

A soft touch on my cheek made me open my eyes. Erik stood just inches away, caressing my face and looking at me like I was the only girl in the world. The pain in his eyes had magnified tenfold, and when his thumb snaked out to trace my bottom lip . . . the whimper that escaped my throat was unavoidable.

I mean, just look at him.

Erik leaned down, pressing his lips to my forehead. "I'll never forget you, either," he murmured. I leaned into the touch, desperate to prolong the contact; the connection; the moment. But much too quickly, his lips were gone. When our eyes met, he'd once again schooled his face into that impassive mask—the one that would serve him well as chief of Valkyris.

But right then, the only thing it was doing was breaking my heart.

"Stand beside me and hold the dagger. This is the spot where my mother manifested Valkyris—I believe it's somehow tied to the blade's magic, and if we can tap into that resonance—"

"We'll be able to activate the dagger. I guess that makes sense. I couldn't get it to do anything on my own, but if this is sacred ground . . ." I shrugged.

"We need to hurry. Last night, our border guards

captured another member of Clan Bjorn. Whoever's feeding them intelligence is still at it, and I don't want this dagger exposed for any longer than absolutely necessary."

It would be a quick send-off then.

It's probably better that way.

"Right." I drew my shoulders back, reached into my cloak, and pulled three letters from the inside pocket. Handing them to Erik, I forced myself to keep my tone light. "I'm not the best at goodbyes, so I wrote these last night. I wanted to thank your parents." I nodded at the stack. The one with Freia and Halvar's names was right on top. "And my friends—give that one to Helene or Katrin, whichever you see first. It's for both of them. And—"

The lump in my throat grew. I swallowed it down and blurted, "The last one's for you."

That haunted look shadowed Erik's face again. He blinked it away, but not before I'd caught the hint of moisture in his eyes.

I can't do this.

But I had to. Erik was right; war was coming. And despite my impressive learning curve, excellent archery skills, and sincere belief in the mission of these awe-inspiring people, my presence would be a distraction at best . . . and a liability, at worst.

I will do this.

I stepped into Erik's space, my chest brushing against his as I reached down and gripped the hilt of the dagger. He wrapped his hands over mine, pressed his lips to my forehead one more time, and simply said, "Home."

This was it. The moment I'd be ripped out of this world and dropped back into mine.

Without thinking, I raised myself onto my tiptoes, stretching as high as I could. I wasn't quite tall enough to reach Erik's lips, but I managed to plant a kiss on the coarse hairs along his jaw before a fierce tingling erupted in my hands. I pulled back, staring wide-eyed at the Viking who'd somehow managed to work his way firmly into my heart, as a thick, gold dust snaked from the dagger. It wrapped itself around my hands, trailing up my forearm in a shimmering, golden mist.

"Goodbye," I whispered.

The agony in Erik's eyes nearly broke me.

The vibrations in my hands intensified, and I knew I was about to be sucked out of Valkyris forever. I clung to Erik's gaze, refusing to break eye contact until the last possible second. I wanted to remember his face —the clarity in his gaze, the square set of his jaw, the way his golden waves framed the most exquisite face I'd ever seen. If this was my final moment with Erik, I was going to make sure I remembered it forever.

You're one in a million, Muscles. I only wish we'd had more time . . .

Ouch!

A sharp jolt rocked my hands. When I tore my gaze away from Erik's, the golden dust around my arms had disappeared. The dagger lay still in my hands, its magic seemingly gone.

"What happened?" I blurted.

"I don't know. I've never used it before. Maybe it takes a few tries?" Erik wrapped my hands around the hilt again, and repeated, "Home."

Nothing.

"Take Saga home," he tried again.

I squeezed my eyes shut.

"Home," I begged. "Please, take me home."

"The future," Erik amended. "Return Saga to the future."

I opened my eyes. My hands were completely and totally normal. No vibrations. No gold dust. No magic.

"Erik," I whispered. "It's not working."

His hair tumbled against his shoulders. "Home," he repeated. "Travel. Transport. Magic." He threw his head back and roared. "Take Saga *home!*"

But the words dissolved into the air. Erik was the heir to a vast, Viking empire. He was a feared warrior, and the face of a forward-thinking civilization. But none of that mattered to the dagger. It remained motionless in my grasp.

"Nothing," I said. "It's doing . . . nothing."

Erik lowered his head. "I don't understand."

My chest tightened. "So, what do we do?"

"I don't know," he admitted. "Saga, I'm sorry. This is the sacred spot. The dagger was activated. It should have taken you home."

Oh, God. Oh God, oh God, oh God.

Leaving Erik was the last thing I'd wanted, but it would have been the right thing to do. I wasn't from here. I didn't belong here. This plan had been my only hope. And now that it had failed . . .

"I'm trapped?" I whispered.

Erik stared at me, denial breaking across his perfect face. "No. We'll find a way to get you back. We'll go to my mother, and demand that—"

"That what? You said it yourself. We're in the right spot. We said the right things. The magic was activated. It just . . . it just said no." I dropped to my knees, not caring that I was on top of a snow-covered hill; that my dress was getting wet; that the island was slowly coming to life, and I'd soon be surrounded by warriors and farmers and dragon riders. The only thing I could think about was the fact that my choices had been completely and totally stripped away. I was trapped in a world facing imminent war, separated from my family by a thousand years, and head over heels for a guy who'd done everything in his power to make sure we never saw each other again.

The final realization hit me like a boulder. Erik had been the one to get the dagger; to locate the sacred spot; to activate the magic. In those final moments, he hadn't asked me to stay—hadn't said he had feelings for me at all—only that he felt responsible for my being here. All these weeks I'd started to fall for him, and when it came down to it . . .

Now I was trapped with him—trapped with a people whose lives were a million times removed from my own. And there was absolutely nothing I could do about it.

I lowered my face to my hands, and I sobbed.

CHAPTER 26

"SAGA." ERIK'S ARMS WOUND around my back, sweeping me firmly into his grasp. "Please, don't cry. I'll find a way out of this."

"How?" I wailed.

"I don't know, but with Odin as my witness, I *will* get you home."

"You want me to leave." I buried my face in his chest. The thick fibers of his cloak were already damp from my tears. What did a few more matter?

"No!" he said fiercely. "I don't. But you do."

I gave way to a fresh bout of tears. I didn't know what I wanted anymore.

"You didn't ask to come here. You had a life before Valkyris, and I will do everything within my power to give that life back to you. I promise you that."

I clung to Erik's arms, my fingernails digging into his cloak. "I'm scared."

"I know." His lips moved lightly against my hair. He

pressed his palms against my back, drawing me into his warmth. With each sniffle, his now-familiar scent filled my head, and eventually the flow of tears slowed. Erik held me until my shoulders stopped shaking—whether it was a minute or an hour, I couldn't tell. The only things I knew for sure were:

1. I was trapped a thousand years in the past, with little hope of ever going home. And,
2. I was wrapped in the arms of the most absurdly gorgeous Viking to have ever walked the face of the Earth.

Maybe my old life was overrated.

I pried my face from Erik's chest, permitting myself one final sniffle before wiping my nose on the back of my sleeve. Two fingers gently nudged at my chin, and my face was being lifted. Erik's beard, then his lips, and finally his eyes came into view, blurry at first, but clearing as I blinked away my tears. He moved his fingers to my cheek, drying the moisture with the pad of his thumb before cupping my jaw in his massive palm. His eyes bored into mine, and the intensity within their clear blue depths made my breath hitch. He was so strong, and so fierce, and so . . . Erik.

A sigh parted my lips, and he shifted his gaze to my mouth. A low rumble sounded through Erik's chest. The vibrations stirred something inside of me, and before I could stop myself, I reached up and stroked his cheek. His beard was coarse against my fingertips, its roughness contrasting the gentle caress of his thumb on my face. He leaned lightly into my touch, his eyes never leaving my mouth. Without thinking, I pressed myself against him, so only the fabric of our cloaks separated us. In that moment he was my rock—the only thing anchoring me to this insanely unbelievable world. And I didn't want *anything* between us. Not even the air.

I'd barely finished the thought when Erik's hand shifted. He laced his fingers through my hair and pulled me to him, crushing his lips against mine in a movement that left me absolutely breathless. It wasn't a tentative first kiss. This kiss was demanding, consuming. Erik claimed my mouth as if he were conquering a foreign land, his lips moving against mine with such fierce determination I knew he'd wanted this every bit as much as I had. His tongue danced with mine, exploring every inch of my mouth as I shifted my hand to the back of his head and pulled him closer. A moan ripped from his throat, and before I knew what was happening, Erik's lips were gone.

No!

A second later, my body all but exploded with pleasure as the Viking licked the delicate skin behind my ear. A shiver wracked my torso, and I lowered my head to give Erik better access. Rough fingertips swept my hair from my neck, and Erik moved upward, flicking my earlobe with his tongue in a move that made staying upright impossible. I swayed, and Erik's hands slipped up my cloak, pressing me to his chest as he ripped his own cloak from his back and flung it onto the ground.

"If you want me to stop, now's the time to tell me." Erik kept me close as he lowered me carefully onto the snow. The full weight of his body pressed against me as he touched his forehead to mine and murmured, "Because I want all of you, Saga Skånstad. For as long as you'll have me."

Oh. My. God.

My self-control imploded as Erik flexed his hips. "Don't stop," I whispered, throwing my arms around his back and drawing him even closer. His mouth slammed into mine and he ran one hand along my ribcage, sending a fresh wave of pleasure rocketing through me. His fingers paused at my hip, then slipped along the edge of my butt before squeezing lightly. He pressed against me again, making what little blood was left in my extremities fly straight to the point of contact. A slow throb pulsed inside of me, building to a point of near pain.

Holy freaking mother.

I was seconds away from begging him to hike up my skirt and just take me already, when he broke contact, rolling onto his back to lie beside me.

"We'd better slow down," he murmured.

"I'm sorry, what?" I panted.

"One more minute, and I wouldn't have been able to stop myself."

"And I am totally fine with that." I'd have preferred

our first time *not* be on a cloak in a snowbank, but at this point I was extremely not picky.

"Oh, are you?" Erik arched a brow.

"Yes." I rolled onto my stomach, propping myself up on my forearms. "I didn't ask you to stop."

"You shouldn't have to." Erik reached up to tuck an errant strand of hair behind my ear. "It's my duty to look after *you*."

Wait. What?

"Yeah . . . that's kind of different where I'm from."

"Well, you're here now." Erik rested his hand on the small of my back. "And here, we take care of our women."

It was the *taking care of* I wanted him to make good on. *Like, immediately.*

"So . . . we're slowing down?" It came out whinier than I meant for it to.

"We'll follow the proper customs, yes."

Dang it.

"What exactly does that entail—dating a Viking?"

Erik's eyes twinkled, and I reached up to trace his pale, pink lips with one finger. He immediately took it into his mouth and sucked, making me moan.

"If by dating you mean courtship, then I'm not going to tell you. But I suggest you prepare yourself, Saga Skånstad. You're in for one hell of a ride."

He returned his attention to my finger, and I dropped my cheek to his shoulder, biting my bottom lip to keep from moaning again.

I had no doubt he'd make good on that promise.

CHAPTER 27

THE TWO MONTHS FOLLOWING *that kiss*
passed in a blur. I'd resumed my classes at
Viking Academy with a slight change in schedule—at
Erik's insistence, I'd enrolled in an additional combat
course and agreed to twice-weekly private training
sessions. And, at my own insistence, I'd added on
Survival and Subterfuge. If I was going to be around
for a war, I was determined to do everything in my
power to see that I was on the winning side.

We'd spoken to Freia about the dagger, and after
she'd gotten over the shock of finding out she'd
summoned me *from the future,* she'd assured us that we
had done everything right. Maybe the dagger's magic
had run out, or the gods weren't inclined to grant me a
return ticket. Either way, it looked like I was here to
stay. But Erik promised he'd keep trying. He was
adamant that I be given a choice. What I did with it
would be up to me.

Axel still hadn't returned. He'd sent word a few weeks back that security in Bjorn was really tight, and he was staying on-site to look out for his troops—the code name he used for Ingrid and Vidia. But we hadn't heard from him since, and we were starting to get worried. Again.

Beyond stressing about Axel, war, and the as-of-now dysfunctional dagger, I kept busy trying to adjust to my new reality. Since calendars as I knew them weren't in existence yet, I didn't notice my eighteenth birthday had passed until the castle began preparing for the winter ball, which would be held a few weeks after the longest day of the year. Since solstice fell in December where I came from, I became an official adult weeks before I realized the big day had come and gone.

Yay, adulting.

I shared my news with Erik as we wiped down our swords after a particularly grueling workout.

"You mean to tell me where you come from, you aren't considered an adult until eighteen?" Erik furrowed his brow. "How do you fill your armies?"

"It works." I shrugged. "And before you ask, no, I'm not an old maid where I come from, either. People there don't get married until they're, like, thirty."

Erik shook his head. "Your world is very strange."

"Back at you." I stood on tiptoe to hang my sword, and turned to Erik with a smile.

"Regardless. Happy birthday, *min kjære*. Clearly, we'll need to celebrate your official entry into adulthood. How are birthdays marked where you come from?"

"Mormor always baked me a chocolate cake, and my cousins would come over, and we'd eat a ton of ice cream."

"Ice cream?" Erik tilted his head.

"Oh, God, we have *got* to get your explorers to discover ice cream. And coffee. Maybe that's why I'm here—to improve your quality of life through food."

"Possibly." Erik hung his sword before snaking an arm around my lower back. "Though I like to think you're here for other reasons."

"Oh, yeah?" I reached up to trail my fingers along his bare chest. Erik preferred to train shirtless, a life choice I had zero issue with. "And what would those be?"

"Devising a defensive infrastructure, for one. I saw the schematics you drew up for reinforcing Valkyris East, and I must say—I'm impressed." Erik widened his stance, halving the full foot differential in our heights. "And giving my cousin someone other than me to obsess over Zaan with—she nearly drove me mad before I agreed to sneak into the headmistress's office and change his course schedule."

"So, *you're* the reason they're lab partners. Helene owes you, big time."

"She does." Erik lowered his forehead to mine. "And then there's the matter of you keeping me company . . ."

"Mmm." My knees weakened as he nipped lightly at my bottom lip. He tightened his grip around my back, pulling me closer so my waist pressed firmly against his. What little blood remained in my head rushed due south, settling just below my navel. I stood on tiptoe so our hips were aligned perfectly. Erik's groan let me know he didn't mind in the slightest, and I slid my palms down his chest, raking my fingernails across the defined abdominal muscles that had spent the past hour taunting me. Training with Erik was a master class in self-restraint. I got to spend the entirety of our sessions ogling his naked chest, but I was never permitted to touch him.

But now . . .

I sighed as Erik's tongue parted my lips. It moved against mine while the hand not holding my back snaked slowly down my bare arm. His palm settled on my butt, and when he hiked me against him, I couldn't stop my moan. We hadn't gone all the way yet—apparently that was *strongly* frowned upon in polite Viking society, owing to unreliable contraception and the plethora of blood feuds spurred by pregnancies out of wedlock. But I didn't have any local family to feud on my behalf, and odds were slim Mormor would ever find out. And when Erik did that nibbling thing on my ear . . .

"Will you just take me up to your room already?" I groaned. "I promise I'll be *really* quiet."

Erik's throaty chuckle vibrated against my neck. "When I finally take you to my room, you will most definitely *not* be quiet."

Oh. My. God.

I threaded my fingers through Erik's hair and pulled his mouth to mine. I'd just decided to plead my case again when the wail of a horn made me jump. It was different from the long wake-up horn—now, three short blasts were followed by one long one. The pattern was near-deafening, as if it had been magically amplified to blast every room at top volume. And it made Erik's spine go completely and totally rigid.

"The alarm." He pulled his lips from mine.

I reluctantly released him. "Is this a good alarm or a bad alarm?"

"Bad one."

Skit.

Erik reached for the wall and retrieved two swords. He held one out to me, then thought better of it and pulled one of the bows from the opposite wall. I grabbed a quill of arrows, and snatched the sword from his hands. If we were weaponing up, I was going to be doubly prepared.

"What's it mean?" I threw my cloak around my shoulders and sheathed my sword.

"It means we're in trouble." Erik grabbed his tunic from the ground and ushered me through the door. "Valkyris has been invaded."

❄

We tore through the castle, Erik throwing on his tunic as he ran. Chaos erupted all around us, doors opening and people suiting up as they charged for what I could only assume were their battle stations. In all my strategy classes, we'd never once talked about security on the island—our border guards and the warriors at Valkyris East were supposed to keep anyone from finding us. How had someone gotten through?

"I don't suppose you'd stay in the castle if I asked you to?" Since we were running, Erik's words were clipped.

"One of the intruders may already have breached the castle," I pointed out. "I'm safest wherever you are."

Erik grimaced. "Stay well behind the front lines. If the riders attack, keep yourself out of the reach of dragon fire. And for Odin's sake, don't die."

"Wasn't planning on it." I held tight to my bow, and pulled an arrow from the quill at my back. I was still a far more effective archer than a swordswoman, and if Erik wanted me behind the front lines I'd be more useful with a bow, anyway.

"If the intruders take the island, find one of the dragons and fly the hell out of here. They've been trained for evacuation drills, and they'll take you to a safe house. I'll know where to look for you." Erik pushed through the back door of the castle, and charged across the snow.

I loped uneasily after him, my sword swinging against my hip. "I have no idea how to fly a dragon," I called.

"Hold on real tight." Erik hung a right at the Drage-hus, and sprinted for the beach. "And whatever you do, don't fall off."

It would be trial by fire, then. *Dragon fire.*

Erik slowed to a jog as he neared the shore. Fierce waves lapped at the island, their grey–blue shade indicating a storm was brewing. A slew of Valkyris warriors took their places on the beach alongside Erik, each staring at the horizon with their swords at their hips. Some were male, but I noticed a solid representation of female fighters alongside the men. Steely determination lined *everyone's* faces.

Here we go.

As I stepped closer to Erik, a gust whipped my cloak across my body. "Now what do we do?"

"Status?" Erik barked at the warrior on his right.

The man pointed two fingers at the sea. "The western watchman reported a single ship bearing Bjorn's banner sailing through the passage. He shot a full two quills of arrows, but the winds were unusually unfavorable. And the dragons refused to engage it."

Good Lord. If the dragons were afraid of whatever was coming, we were completely and totally screwed.

Erik raised a fist, signaling his troops to hold. "The dragons wouldn't fire on the ship?"

"No, sir."

So screwed.

At that moment, the blood-red sail of a midsized ship appeared on the horizon. The boat sailed steadily toward us, wavering with each fresh gale of wind. A storm was definitely coming in. It was going to be a big one.

I ripped an arrow from my quiver and readied my

bow. But Erik's raised fist held my fire. "Look at that ship," he murmured. "It's barely controlled—either its seamen are injured, or . . ."

"Or they're inexperienced." I lowered my bow, and squinted at the boat. It barreled toward Valkyris, its speed far too high for a safe approach. If it didn't slow down, it was going to crash.

Maybe that was the plan?

"Erik!" I cried. "They're going to hit us."

"*Skit.* Everyone, clear a path," Erik ordered. "When the ship grounds, we'll seize its occupants."

"It's not a kill mission?" The warrior to Erik's right lowered his sword.

Erik narrowed his eyes. "I haven't decided."

We retreated to the higher ground, the seconds ticking by as the ship drew closer. Clan Bjorn's banner flapped fiercely in the wind, but something didn't feel right. Valkyris was supposed to be unlocatable—how had Bjorn found us after all of these years? Moreover, if these really were the barbaric, brutal warriors come to kill us, why weren't they already launching their assault?

Or at least putting up their shields?

When the ship was a hundred yards out, I noticed its occupants' flailing arms, and caught the voices shouting above the waves. A hoarse male called out navigational instructions—ones that clearly weren't being followed—while a female's warbled scream betrayed her terror. "Don't kill us! Please! We're not intruders!"

"Don't shoot!" the male added. "It's us!"

Erik's eyes narrowed. "That sounds like—"

"We're going to crash," another female shrieked. "Oh, my gods!"

"It could be a trap." Erik shook his head. "Keep your weapons at the ready and wait for my orders."

But my bow had dropped to my side, shock reverberating from my ears to my feet. I'd have known that voice anywhere. It had sung me to sleep, soothed my terrified tears, and given me the encouragement I'd needed when I'd thought my life had reached its breaking point. It was a voice I'd never forget . . . and one I hadn't expected to ever hear again.

"No way," I whispered. I threw my bow to the ground and jogged toward the water.

"Saga!" Erik's arm snaked out, hooking mine and pulling me back. "What are you doing?"

I wrenched my arm free. "Erik, call off your warriors. They need us."

"Who needs us? Saga, what's going on?"

"Help! Oh, gods! Aieeeee!" The cry pierced the air, panic echoing across the beach as the ship dredged through the shallows. The crack of splintered wood was punctuated with the fierce whoosh of a wave as the ship crashed on the shore. Thumps and groans emanated from the boat as bodies were thrown together. The ship was still lurching from side to side when a disheveled redhead popped over the edge of the boat. Wild, green eyes scanned the shore, widening as they roved over the bevy of Valkyris warriors.

"Please don't shoot!" the girl blurted. "I come in peace. And I have your Axel!"

"Ingrid!" I cried out.

"Saga?" She leapt from the boat, wading through the shallow water. The too-bulky dress of the Clan Bjorn slaves slowed her movements. "Oh, my gods, it's you!"

"How did you escape?" I reached the edge of the water and charged right in, not caring that it was freezing, or that I'd probably just ruined my only pair of boots. "Oh, Ingrid—I'm so glad you're okay!"

Ingrid launched herself at me, enveloping me in wild red curls. "I am *not* okay. I've been on a boat for two weeks with Vidia, who it turns out has terrible ocean sickness, and Axel, who claims he was sent to rescue us, but has ended up being far more trouble than he's worth."

I craned my neck to see into the boat.

"Saga." Erik's low growl came from the shore. "If you don't tell me what's going on right this minute, I'm going to lose my mind."

"Sorry! This is Ingrid—my friend from Clan Bjorn. The one you sent Axel after."

Ingrid lifted her hand in a wave. "*Hei.*"

Erik gave a tight nod. "I still need to search the boat."

"Erik!" I placed my hand on my hip.

"It's protocol." He directed three of his warriors to oversee the inspection.

"Sorry about him." I turned to Ingrid.

"No. He's right to be careful." Ingrid clasped my

hands in hers. "Let's get Vidia and Axel off the ship—preferably to a healer if you have one. And then you and I need to talk."

Oh, God. "Okay."

"The boat's clean," one of the warriors called out. "But Axel is wounded. And the maiden is . . . unwell." He paled as Vidia sat up, leaning over the edge of the boat to puke.

"Bring them to the healing unit, and see that their injuries are tended to. Then alert the rest of the island that we're not under attack. Though we'll need to increase security on the western watch." Erik barked his orders while I guided Ingrid out of the water. We stood on the shore as the warriors helped Vidia and Axel off the boat.

"Oh, Vidia." I shook my head. "I'm so sorry—we'll get you fixed up."

"I'm just happy to be off that gods-forsaken boat," she moaned. "Is it really safe here?"

"It is," I assured. "I promise."

"Thank gods," she whispered. Then she leaned over and puked all over her shoes. *Poor thing.*

"Take her to the healing unit *immediately.* See to it that she's adequately hydrated," Erik ordered. "We'll follow shortly."

"Good Lord, Axel. What happened to you?" I winced at the gaping wound on Axel's right arm. The gash was a full five inches long, and framed by a horrifyingly vivid bruise. A bloodied piece of cloth hung from what used to be his sleeve.

"Clan Bjorn is no joke." Axel limped toward me.

"You need to see a healer." Erik held out his arm. "I'll take you."

"That can wait." Axel winced as he clutched his arm, seemingly overcome by a fresh wave of pain. "This can't. Saga, Erik—you need to hear what Ingrid has to say."

Oh, God.

Ingrid squeezed my hands. Her eyes flickered from me to Erik as she spoke. "You humiliated Lars and Olav at the *Ting*. They swore they'd track down your tribe and make you pay, even though nobody's been able to find Valkyris for . . . we don't even know how long you've been in existence."

"Good," Erik said.

"Well, someone approached Lars after you left the *Ting*—they said they'd sell information about your tribe on the condition that, if they were ever found out, they'd be made a leader in Clan Bjorn. Lars took the deal. He sent two scouts with the spy, and waited for news. But the scouts never returned."

Erik's eyes shot venom. "I killed them."

"Actually, *I* killed them," Axel corrected.

I ignored them both, and focused on Ingrid. "Continue."

"That would have been the end of it, but Axel arrived just as Vidia and I were *finally* about to escape. We'd taken the arrows from where you told us we'd find them—decomposing bears are disgusting, by the way—and we'd stolen enough supplies to support

271

ourselves for a few weeks. We were a day away from making a run for it, when *he* showed up." Ingrid jabbed her thumb toward Axel.

"And your life became infinitely better for it." Axel grinned through his pain.

"To be determined." Ingrid rolled her eyes. "Anyway, he told us he was with you, Saga—and that if we helped him, he'd make sure we had a home where you lived. Of course, at that point we thought you'd been taken by brutish thugs, so I did what you told me and . . . um . . ."

"She shot me!" Axel exploded. "She. Shot. Me! And of course, Erik sent me with *no healer*, so I had to extract the arrowheads myself. Hurt like a mother-freaking—"

"I said I was sorry!" Ingrid shouted back. "And I steered all the way here, so you wouldn't make your injury worse."

"I still had to row the bloody ship!" Axel yelled.

I covered my smile while they bickered. I knew the dagger had gifted me some magical inner-ear translator when it had dropped me here—one that most definitely modernized its language. But Axel and Ingrid's back and forth was so refreshingly normal— even if the subject matter wasn't—that for a minute I felt like I was back in high school, watching my cousin bicker with her crush.

Wonder how things will play out with these two . . .

"Enough arguing," Erik interrupted. "Axel, you

probably deserved to be shot. Ingrid, continue with your story."

"Thank you," Ingrid huffed. "The short of it is, once Axel convinced us he wasn't a thug, Vidia and I agreed to help him. We talked to the thralls who were working the *Ting* tents, and we passed on the information we could gather. But the spy didn't show up again . . . and after a while, Lars became suspicious. He put us on lockdown, and when Axel couldn't reach us, well." She pointed to the assassin's right arm.

"Of course, I came for them." Axel sighed. "And of course, it was a trap."

"Axel." I cringed. "What happened?"

"Well, the girls are here, so it ended fine. But those monsters killed my dragon. And banged up my arm pretty bad."

The remaining warriors gasped. Murmurs of, "They killed a dragon?" rocked the beach.

"Is that really bad?" I whispered to Erik.

"Not only is it extremely difficult to kill a dragon— which means our enemy has either skill or weapons exceeding what we previously believed—but it's a violation of the covenant between man and the gods." He exhaled heavily. "Dragons are sacred."

Oh.

"That's why we had to sail, instead of flying. Since Axel was rowing mostly one-armed, and Vidia and I had never steered a ship before . . ." Ingrid shrugged. "It was rough."

"How'd you steal a ship from Clan Bjorn?" I was impressed.

"We'd found an herb in the forest that Vidia recognized from her old tribe. Apparently, it knocks people out for hours." Ingrid's emerald eyes flashed. "Another thrall snuck it into Lars' stew for us, and we had our window to escape."

Pride filled my chest, and I beamed at Erik. "I told you they were amazing."

"That you did." Erik rubbed the back of his neck. "Well, I guess we'd better get you settled in the castle. You're probably going to want rooms near Saga's, so I'll have someone check on the availability in the academy wing, and—"

"She's not done," Axel interjected. "The bad part's coming."

Skit.

Ingrid wrung her fingers together. "Before we drugged Lars, we overheard him talking with his warriors. He was *really* angry about what happened at the *Ting*."

"I gathered," I said drily.

"No, *really* angry. He was counting on his scouts to come back with information on how to find this place, and when they didn't . . ." She shook her head. "It wasn't good."

Erik glowered. "What does he want?"

Ingrid turned to me, worry lines framing her eyes. "He wants you back, Saga. He wants Erik dead. And he wants Valkyris destroyed. And . . ."

"And?" I held my breath.

"And he's vowed he'll kill anyone who stands in his way."

My. God.

An angry growl ripped from Erik's throat. "He'll never lay a finger on Saga."

"He won't get close enough to even try." Axel cracked his knuckles.

"Niklas," Erik barked at one of the remaining warriors. "Send half a battalion to the western border, and another to the east. Asta, see that the riders double patrols—I want a dragon in the air at all times. The rest of you, report to the war room for further instructions. And Saga—" Erik's voice cracked as he faced me.

"I'll be okay," I lied. My stomach had commenced Olympic-level gymnastics routines, and my heart thundered like a pack of terrified rhinos. But Erik's eyes carried enough panic—I didn't want to add to his worry.

"*Jævla* right you'll be okay. You and I are moving to twice-daily trainings. Swords in the morning, hand-to-hand at night. I'm not going to lose you."

My rhino herd heart melted at the words. "No." I smiled. "You're not."

Erik nodded once before ushering us toward the castle. He held out his hand as he walked, and as I fell into step beside him, I laced my fingers through his. I took what comfort I could in his focused determination.

I was a thousand years from Mormor and Olivia

and the only life I'd ever known. I was being hunted by a vitriolic Viking. And I'd just agreed to two-a-days with the least sympathetic trainer in the history of ever.

I snuck a glance at Erik, whose barely contained fury was etched on every inch of his beautiful face. He looked down at me and winked, a thousand words packed into the silent communication. He had my back. He always had . . . and as crazy as it sounded, maybe he always would.

I squeezed Erik's hand and marched determinedly at his side. In that moment I was safe—harbored by a tribe that was improving the world one small step at a time, and educated by a school that challenged its students to be the best possible version of themselves. I was surrounded by friends who looked out for each other every bit as much as my family had. And I had a partner who was prepared to do everything in his power to ensure not only that I was protected, but that *I didn't need protecting*. As uncertain as my future was, right then I knew that I had every tool I needed to face the challenges that lay ahead.

It would have to be enough.

✳

How to Viking
by Saga Skånstad

1. Learn all the things.

2. Don't brag once you learn all the things—everybody else knows all the things, too.
3. Do for yourself all that is in your power to do. But at the same time . . .
4. Support others.
5. Say yes to adventure.
6. Try not to lose your heart to the Valkyris heir. *(Too late!)*

VIKING ACADEMY'S LEFSE RECIPE

(FLOUR VERSION)

1 egg
½ cup sugar
¼ cup butter (room temperature)
1 cup milk
4 cups flour
½ tsp baking powder

Whip eggs with sugar and butter. Stir in milk.
Mix baking powder and flour. Add to wet ingredients.
Add additional flour as needed until dough is soft, but
not too sticky.
Roll out lefse to desired thickness. Cook in a frying pan
or a griddle over high heat.
Serve with butter, cinnamon, and sugar.

Take a picture and share it with me!

The Academy crew returns in
VIKING ACADEMY: VIKING CONSPIRACY

Trapped in a world she never knew existed, Saga Skån-stad throws herself into her new life at Viking Academy. She learns to scale icy mountains, shoot flaming arrows, and ride on the back of a particularly ill-tempered dragon. But when Erik abruptly disappears, and the true reason for Saga's arrival in his world is unveiled, her fears only increase—not just for herself, but for the Viking who's captured her heart.

When a surprise attack threatens her new home, Saga quickly realizes her life is on the line. Valkyris' enemies are determined to bring down her clan, destroy its heir, and force her into a living nightmare. Saga will do whatever it takes to preserve the world her friends have worked so hard to build. But her choice may cost her the life she never knew she wanted . . . and a love she never could have imagined.

ACKNOWLEDGMENTS

To my amazing, inspiring, adventurous little family—I'm so grateful God gave me you.

To Lauren Clarke and her team at CREATING ink, whose sharp eyes and kind hearts always bring out the best in our Norse crews. To Mariana, for keeping the Viking ship afloat. To Laura and Lorna, the dynamic beta-duo/sounding board. And to Alison, for *all* the kitchen table pep talks. Bless you guys.

To the readers who dream across the realms with me. I continue to be humbled by your support. I couldn't do this without you.

To everyone who fights for fairness, who celebrates love, and who believes in fairies—thank you for making our world a brighter place. Never, *ever* change.

And to MorMorMa. For everything.

ABOUT THE AUTHOR

Before finding domestic bliss in suburbia, internationally bestselling author S.T. Bende lived in Manhattan Beach (became overly fond of Peet's Coffee) and Europe...where she became overly fond of McVitie's cookies. Her love of Scandinavian culture and a very patient Norwegian teacher inspired her YA Norse fantasy books. And her love of a galaxy far, far away inspired her to write children's books for Star Wars. She hopes her characters make you smile, and she dreams of skiing on Jotunheim and Hoth.

Learn more about the world of S.T. Bende at
www.stbende.com.

Meet Axel's not-so-mythical Asgardian relation in
THE ÆRE SAGA: PERFEKT ORDER

All's fair when you're in love with War.

For seventeen-year-old Mia Ahlström, a world ruled by order is the only world she allows. A lifetime of chore charts, to-do lists and study schedules have helped earn her a spot at Redwood State University's engineering program. And while her five year plan includes finding her very own happily-evah-aftah, years at an all-girls boarding school left her feeling woefully unprepared for keg parties and co-ed extracurricular activities.

So nothing surprises her more than catching the eye of Tyr Fredriksen at her first college party. The imposing Swede is arrogantly charming, stubbornly overprotective, and runs hot-and-cold in ways that defy reason… until Mia learns that she's fallen for the Norse God of War; an immortal battle deity hiding on Midgard (Earth) to protect a valuable Asgardian treasure from a feral enemy. With a price on his head, Tyr brings more than a little excitement to Mia's rigidly controlled life. Choosing Tyr may be the biggest distraction—or the greatest adventure—she's ever had.

Learn more about the world of S.T. Bende at www.stbende.com.